FIELD CHOICE

A NOVEL BY RICK NORMAN

FIELDER'S CHOICE

A NOVEL BY RICK NORMAN

AUGUST HOUSE PUBLISHERS, INC.

LITTLE ROCK

Published by August House, Inc.,
P.O. Box 3223, Little Rock, Arkansas, 72203,
501-372-5450.

Printed in the United States of America
10 9 8 7 6 5 4 3

LIBRARY OF CONGRESS
CATALOGING-IN-PUBLICATION DATA

Norman, Rick J.
Fielder's choice : a novel / by Rick Norman — 1st ed.
        p.   cm.
ISBN 0-87483-172-5 (acid-free): $17.95
ISBN 0-87483-204-7 (acid-free): $9.95
I. Title.
PS3564.0634F54   1991
813'.54—dc20   90-21799

First Published 1991
First Paperback Edition, 1992

Executive: Liz Parkhurst
Project editor: Judith Faust
Cover design: Byron Taylor
Typography: Lettergraphics, Little Rock

This book is printed on archival-quality paper which meets
the guidelines for performance and durability of the
Committee on Production Guidelines for Book Longevity
of the Council on Library Resources.

AUGUST HOUSE, INC.   PUBLISHERS   LITTLE ROCK

To the Jimmy St. Vrains, John Andersons, Fred
Merkles, Heinie Zimmermans,
Mickey Owens, Billy Loeses, and
Bill Buckners of the world;
if not forgiven, may their mistakes
be mercifully forgotten.

I began playing baseball—and, thank the Lord, retired from the St. Louis Browns—before designated hitters, batting helmets or gloves, exploding scoreboards, artificial turf, and prima donna ballplayers with pants tighter than Mikhail Bulge-itnikov's. We worried about bean-balls because they could kill us, not because they might muss our mousse.

The ballclub was like my family, and during the 1941 season, Gooseball Fielder was like my little brother. We roomed together both on the road and in St. Louis at the Coronado Hotel. He was a young pup fresh out of some little high school somewhere in Arkansas or Mississippi and green as the outfield at Sportsman's Park.

Being from New Orleans myself, I had seen it all at least twice and done most of it once. I tried to help him as much as I could, but I didn't have very long to work with him.

After the war, we heard Gooseball had gotten into some bad trouble with Uncle Sam. The Browns' management let it be known we ought to steer clear of him.

It was a true joy for me to read this book and find out, after almost fifty years, what Gooseball thought of that '41 season, what happened to him because of the war, and exactly how and why I had been poisoned on a road trip to Mexico.

Thomas M. "Neckless" Womack
St. Louis Browns 1931-1947

1

This ain't about aiding and abetting the enemy, Major. It's about the 1941 American League pennant. I can't believe after all this world has been through in the last five years that somebody is trying to go back and change the score. Or maybe settle one.

I appreciate you agreeing to take a look at my case. I didn't realize until I got served with the papers yesterday that someone's been holding up my discharge. I figured when I got out of the hospital in San Francisco, I would never have to salute nobody again.

I want to tell you up front that I *did* more than likely say to Colonel Cole I was gonna "play ball," but I never said "with the Japanese." And I did learn a Japanese boy how to thow my gooseball, but not too good before he went and killed hisself. Or maybe his pappy killed him, I don't know. But I swear to you I never told nobody no war secrets. They trying to take a few bad pitches and make me out a bad pitcher.

When you're growing up, they teach you right from wrong, good from evil. Is it right to steal a apple or ain't it? Then you find out most times there's more than two choices, and there ain't no little angel whispering to you what to do. Do you thow a fastball? A curve? A slider? Which one's right? The one that don't come back faster than it went in—but that depends on where some other fellow decides to swing his bat, don't it?

I got so bad at making decisions, I quit altogether. If I had no choice but to make a choice, I tried to have something to blame when things went wrong. I used horrorscopes, superstitions, lucky coins, I even used the Bible.

But I ain't ashamed of the choices I made that wound me up here. They might be the first decisions I ever really made. They surely are the first ones I made for the right reasons.

How can them folks believe I aided and abetted the enemy? The Army don't know me. They don't know Colonel Cole, and how he used up men in that prison camp to keep him and his friends fat and happy. They don't know my brother's been a skunk all his life and would do anything to get even with me.

First time I can remember my brother Jude trying to get me killed was when I was about nine. That would have made my brother Jugs ten, and Jude, he'd have been seven. Jugs had made me and him a slingshot out of a forked branch and rubber from a old inner tube. We'd been around Smackover scaring the daylights out of many of God's creatures, and was heading home by way of the backyard when Jugs spied Paw bent over next to the house connecting the hose pipe to the faucet. Before I could stop him, Jugs drawed that inner tube back about five times its length and let a cat eye fly straight at Paw's rear end. I heard the marble hit meat and Paw's headbone hit the side of the house—hard. It was a second or two before Paw bellered.

By the time Paw got his eyes uncrossed, Jugs was headed up the back steps, and there I was, fifteen foot behind, holding the slingshot he'd stuck in my hand, and trying to cry. It took a scream from Maw to bring me to my senses and get my legs rolling. Paw probably would've caught me if Maw hadn't give us another few seconds' grace by latching the screen door.

Jugs and me hid under the bed and Jude sat on the top bunk crying. Just beyond the door to our room we could hear Maw pleading with Paw to spare our young lives. Course Jude hadn't done nothing—he never did—but he knew even at age seven that when Paw popped his top, there wasn't no prisoners taken.

After about ten minutes, the shuffling in the hall died down and the medicine cabinet slammed shut one last time. After half a hour that seemed like a week, there was a soft knock on our door. Paw come in the room and coaxed us out from under the bed. He said, "Boys, you hurt your old Pappy very bad." Jugs and me said we was sorry. Jude said he didn't do it, Jugs done it and Jax—that's me—laughed. See there? Jude started digging his grave with his teeth way before he talked to the Army about me.

Jude's tattling sent Jugs and me scampering back under the bed, but Paw was calm by this time and explained in a slow, steady voice the dangers of playing with a slingshot, the worth of being considerate of others, and all about the soft spot on top of your head that can kill you if you hit it just right. We listened close, nodding when we ought to and watching for any twitching or wrinkling in his forehead. Finally, to drive home his point, Paw turned around and pulled down his overhauls and his boxer shorts to show us the deep blue circle on his behind.

I didn't have time to say I was sorry again before snot shot out of Jugs's nose and he busted out laughing. Well, Paw caught me by the ankle before I could make it all the way under the bed and whupped us three boys with a switch till our bottoms looked like six Jap flags.

Jude always was the odd man out amongst the three of us brothers. And not just for being the youngest and the puniest. He was smart, for one thing. Book smart. But you can be smart and be a all-right fellow, or you can be smart and be peculiar, and Jude was peculiar. I am not just saying that because of what has gone on between us. You call the Smackover operator and get her to connect you with anybody in town. Every single one of them knows how he is, except his own mother.

Jugs was born the oldest. Maw named him Isaac, which means "laughter." Paw give him his nickname young because of the angle of his ears. Said they looked like a couple of jug handles. Old Jugs was the best natural athlete I ever seen, and that includes them I knew in the major leagues.

Growing up, sports was everything to me and Jugs. We lived and breathed sports from can-see to can't-see. Jugs was a four-letter man at Smackover High School. He'd have got more letters if they'd been more sports. He quarterbacked the football team, caught for the baseball team, ran the hurdles and relays, and played forward on the Class-A 1939 High School Championship basketball team. To Jugs, sports wasn't a contest, they was a game. I seen him come up to bat a fourth time in a ballgame, having already got three hits and the pitcher trying to stick one in his ear—he'd be smiling on the way down, and laughing and dusting hisself getting back up. I actually never seen him mad at anybody in his whole life. Which ain't to say he wouldn't get even.

When Jugs was a senior and I was a junior, Bubba Broadax, a big old outlander from a triple-A school in Houston, moved to Smackover in the middle of the year. They was all kind of talk about Bubba and why he'd left Houston. The only facts we knew for sure was that he'd just left and his father was just dead. Rumor was, Bubba had caught him one afternoon after school fooling with Bubba's little sister. I don't guess it was ever decided whether Bubba killed him, his sister killed him, or the old man killed hisself, but we heard Bubba spent the rest of the afternoon cleaning his father's brains off the kitchen ceiling so his mother would be spared that sight when she come home from work. We didn't know if the stories was true, but the talk and the look in his eye made sure we give him plenty of room.

Bubba had started off on the wrong foot. He announced that he'd been the all-district catcher in Houston, Texas, and would be the catcher for our team once the season come. Well, Jugs was in the middle of basketball season and didn't mind him popping off. But me, I was mad. Besides him being my brother, Jugs was my catcher. He had taught me everything I knew about pitching. He had even learned me, more or less, how to thow the gooseball. Big Mr. Houston Texas had another think coming if he thunk he was going to just waltz hisself into a starting job without no trouble from me.

Because Jugs was involved with basketball and track in the spring, Bubba seen a lot of action early on in the season. Soon as track was done, Jugs took over as the number one catcher. Well, that burnt Bubba up. He got even meaner. He cussed the coach, and he cussed Jugs, though not to their faces. I let Jugs know, but I never could get him riled.

Finally, instead of letting the thing fester, which wasn't helping the team, Jugs went to Bubba and apologized for being the number-one catcher. Told him that ever since Coach had seen him catch a baseball thowed off the water tower, Coach thought he was the greatest catcher in the world. Well, Bubba announced to everbody that he could catch a ball thowed off a water tower, or anywheres else, for that matter. I myself never remembered Jugs catching no ball off no water tower. I myself would have doubted somebody catching such a ball. Be about like catching a meteor. That water tower was *tall.*

The tower was next to the field and must've been a hundred foot high, give or take. Right after practice that day, the whole team marched over to it and circled round the ladder. The rules was that Jugs would thow the ball as high as he could off the water tower and Bubba had to catch it on the fly. No second chances.

Jugs was a little late getting to the tower, but we all cheered him as he climbed the old rusty ladder to the top of the tank with the ball down his shirt. Down on the ground, Bubba yelled at us to make sure we give him lots of room. "Spread out, peckerwoods," he says. It was getting dusty-dark, so the sun wouldn't be no problem. Jugs yelled down to us, then rared back and let her fly. The ball seemed like it all but disappeared on the way up. As it started on down, Bubba begun circling. He even started yelling, "I got it! I got it!" like somebody was gone try to rob him of it. In the middle of a "I got it!" he froze and his mouth dropped open. He caught the ball over his head. The force of the ball carried his mitt into his forehead— and the dang thing exploded. Greeny-gray brains flew everwhere. Some of the boys screamed and a couple took off home. I felt sick to my stomach. I hadn't never seen no one's head blow up before.

When we unfroze from the shock, we crept up to Bubba who was laying flat of his back. In his mitt was a little chunk of honeydew melon. Somebody picked up another piece, and it had baseball stitches drawed on the rind. Jugs was laughing so hard he had to stop every rung or two to keep from falling off the ladder. Once we realized it wasn't brains splattered on us, we rolled around under that water tower till dark. It took Bubba a good while before he got up, which he done well before the rest of us. As he come by, he stopped and pointed his finger in my face like it was my fault. I hadn't done nothing but laugh like everbody else, but I stopped laughing fast when I saw that finger.

From then on out, Bubba didn't pop off no more. Matter of fact, I ain't sure he ever talked again till he got growed. But he kept that same look in his eye. He played a good enough right field and led the team in batting. In the war, he was a M.P. in France and supposedly knocked the top of a dogface's head off with a billy club in a cabaret for giving him backjaw. They didn't court martial him, just sent him stateside. He later come home after the War and is now the deputy sheriff of Smackover, and he played his part this week in me being here. But I'm getting ahead of myself.

2

Hard as I tried, the older I got, the more I messed up. In Jugs's last year of high school ball, in nineteen and thirty-nine, we played a do-or-die game for the Class-A championship. I can tell you that coming here to Little Rock to play in that game was the biggest thing in my life up to that time.

The only real bad game I'd ever had was against Arkadelphia back early that season, and it wasn't really my fault, though I guess maybe it was when you look at it close. I had pitched two no-hitters in a row and done got a little big-headed as far as Jugs was concerned. He told me in a nice way that I had the swell-head and was getting right hard to stomach. I told him people just thought I was stuck-up because I was so good.

Now, I had always counted on Jugs for my signals and location, and he was a master at keeping a book in his head on each batter. In this here game against Arkadelphia, I didn't like a couple of the pitches Jugs called, so I started shaking off his signals. Jugs figured I was just trying to show him and everbody else that it was me in control of this fine game I was pitching. Well, not too long after that, they started tagging my gooseball. I quit waving off signals and thowed everything Jugs told me to, but it still didn't help. When our six-run lead was gone, Coach yanked me. I lost that game and about every drop of confidence I ever had right along with it.

Walking home after, Jugs told me not to worry about it. He said the reason I got pounded so good wasn't me picking the wrong pitches. He had been telling the batters exactly what I was going to thow and where.

He said it was better for me to learn a lesson than for us to win a game. I could not believe he would lose the game for everbody just to straighten me out. But then, winning never did mean too much to him: he come to play.

He done right, I guess, because here we come to Little Rock ready to win the state championship trophy. We had to jump-start the old team bus with a tractor to get it going, but it went, and half of Smackover was behind us when we pulled up to the ballfield.

Me being a junior, I was extra excited because Coach had told me I'd start. I had been pitching pretty fair that season if I do say so myself, and there wasn't many could hit my gooseball. Usually, the only ones to make any contact was the bottom of the order, who wouldn't of come close to my slider, much less so my gooseball, except they closed their eyes when they swung.

I pitched good, but we couldn't get but one little run and that was off Bubba's homer in the top of the first. After that, it was mostly three up and three down. In the bottom of the last, I walked a man on a hometown call, and he come on around to third on the only base hit I give up all night.

Now, with a man on first and one on third and no outs, you'd expect the man on first to maybe try to steal second and take away the double play and then fix it so's a base hit would win the game. Every team has a play for this situation, and every kid that plays baseball knows it. It's the one where the catcher acts like he's thowing to second to get the stealer, while all the time he's really trying to draw the runner from third into a rundown. Instead of letting the ball go into second, the pitcher catches the thow and pegs the runner out at home. I knew this play.

Jugs come out in front of the plate and scratched his behind. That was the signal. I seen it. I must have—I was there right in the middle of it.

I taken my stretch. I thew the ball home, heard my first baseman yelling the runner had broke, seen Jugs come up thowing, ducked my head out of the way of the ball so I didn't get it tore off, and watched the ball sail plumb on past second base. The centerfielder was coming up hard, trying to back up a thow that wasn't supposed to ever get that far. He tried hard to get the runner at home, even reached to barehand the ball, but it skidded out into the outfield and both runners scored. The game was over.

Little Rock and Smackover was both staring at me, and there wasn't nowhere to hide. Everbody on the team was reading my pedigree out loud. Jugs come out to the mound and told me my fly was open. It wasn't really, but he got me to look, and I somehow knew I was not going to die nor descend into the bowels of the earth nor get fetched off the mound by a armed escort. So I walked to the bus, and me and Jugs had the back seat all to ourselves.

Nobody said a thing on the bus, not even Jugs. Coach didn't even say nothing when the bus wouldn't crank, though he did turn around and stare at me like I had something to do with it. After the bus got jump-started and we headed home, somebody whispered they had seen Coach crying.

The bus ride back was dark and quiet as a graveyard, except for some sniffling and one or two backfires. Since we was due to arrive in Smackover after midnight, Coach had got a diner to stay open to feed us a late supper. The diner was officially closed, but the owner come out from his house in the back when he heard the bus horn and opened up for us. The parents had all chipped in to buy us what was supposed to be our victory meal: big, juicy steaks. Let me tell you, there was many a night in that POW camp in Japan I would remember them steaks and all the trimmings.

Jugs and me sat at a table by ourselves, though not by choice. Nobody wanted to sit with me because I had lost the game. Nobody wanted to sit with Jugs because they was afraid he'd make them laugh.

When the steaks come out, Jugs got me to take off my pitching jacket. He hung it on the back of a chair and crumpled up some crackers on the plate in front of it. I didn't get it till the owner come around serving the steaks. Jugs told him they was three of us at the table, but the other fellow was in the bathroom washing up. The owner left a steak, and Jugs and me split it.

We was finishing up our steak-and-a-half when Coach, all red-eyed and puffy-faced, gets out of the bus and comes into the diner. It ain't long before him and the owner gets into a shouting match, and then they both start counting heads. Besides me losing the state championship on a bonehead play, my brother had done caused me to eat Coach's victory steak.

Baseball never was as much fun without Jugs on the team. He joined the Navy the day after he graduated. In '39, there wasn't much work around Smackover outside the oil patch, and if the service would take you, it was a good enough job.

The last time Jugs and me played ball together was the next season. Jugs happened to be home on leave when we was playing our serious cross-county rival, Jefferson Davis High. Jugs showed up at the game, which was being played at their park on a sunny Saturday afternoon before as big a crowd as I ever seen at a regular high school game. Everbody was glad to see Jugs, and he was a picture in his dress whites with his wings showing he was an official naval aviator. Coach asked him would he coach first base, and Jugs obliged.

We was facing a pitcher every bit as good as me, though he looked to be thirty years old. He had a three-day growth every time I ever seen him, and somebody said he had three kids up in the stands. Somebody else said one of his kids was playing second base. Jugs told us he seen him pitching semi-pro. I didn't know what the truth was, but I know that day we couldn't touch him. He was thowing aspirins.

I wasn't much of a batter. I'd caught one in the ear as a youngun, and my batting stance was designed for bailing out, not for power. I always made up my mind before the pitch whether I was swinging or not. I usually picked the odd number or either the even number pitches to swing on. I found it made batting a whole lot easier—and quicker, too.

That day, Coach told us just to hit what we seen, and if we didn't see nothing, to come on back and sit down and be proud that we tried. Jugs give us some good advice, too. He said to use a lighter bat. It wouldn't do us no better batting, but we wouldn't get so tired toting it back and forth from the dugout.

I don't remember if this was our last at bat, but it was pert near over. I don't think nobody had been on base except a couple of pinch runners for the fellows that had been hit in the temple due to sneering at the pitcher or crowding the plate. Since the lime for the batter's box had long since been smeared out by diving batters, I made a point of asking the umpire where was the furtherest place I could stand from homeplate without being out of the batter's box. Even then, I fudged in the interest of safety.

On one of the pitches—either even or odd, whichever I'd picked—I swung and completely by accident knocked a line drive over the centerfielder's head. I tore out running as fast as I could, watching Jugs the whole time. He was motioning me to make my turn and head on to second. He was yelling, "Keep going, Jax! Go on!" I was about ten steps past first base on my way to second when Jugs started hollering, "Get back! Back! Back!" I didn't know what had happened, but when you're running the bases, you don't watch where the ball is, you listen to your coach.

I come back into first, and Jugs tells me to hit the dirt. I slud into first headfirst, scooping up a mouthful of red dust like a steam shovel, and Jugs points a finger to second.

"He missed the ball! He missed it, Jax!" I got up and lit back out for second. I heard him yelling for me to slide.

I'm sliding into second base, and out of the corner of my eye, I see a man in street clothes heading towards second from the third base side. I look up through the cloud of dust I just made, and there stands Coach. He looks down his nose at me and then over at Jugs, who is rolling on the ground in his dress whites, laughing to beat all. In fact, the whole grandstand is giving me the horse laugh. Coach tells me to go sit on the bus. He also thanks Jugs and asks him to go sit in the stands.

The centerfielder had made a great catch on my line drive, and I had been out since about my third step out of the batter's box. Now, I pitched major league ball for the St. Louis Browns, but the people of Jeff Davis County still remember me for the afternoon I tried stretching a fly out into a double.

My big brother was always my hero, but I believe it was that game I begun thinking I might just as well be doing my own thinking.

If my mind wasn't cluttered enough, I had to start worrying about girls. It took me a while after I started worrying about them before I decided to start liking them. In junior high we called a fellow a queer if he liked girls more than baseball, so I had the idea that girls and sports didn't mix.

I wanted more than anything in the world to pitch in the majors, and it seemed like females could only be distracting. Since then, I pitched in the majors and been to war, and I ain't sure I wasn't right to start off with.

There was another reason it took me a long time to get keen on girls. I was very shy and quiet on account of being so bony. One day, I worked up my courage and asked Maw and Paw to tell me the truth whether I was funny-looking, being so skinny and all. Maw says, "Of course not, honey-bunch," which was just what I wanted to hear.

Then Paw says that I shouldn't be worried about my skinny body, what with having a head shaped like a potato. A potato! I couldn't hardly believe it. I never knew exactly what he meant by it, but I can tell you I was never the same afterwards. I wish now I had back all the hours I spent in the bathroom with two and three mirrors trying to look at my head from every which way. That one crack by Paw pretty much undermined my social life until the Japs finished it off.

Jugs wasn't much help with girls neither. Everything was a joke to him. Like the time him and me went on a double date with girls that didn't know one another. Jugs had the idea of telling each girl when we picked her up that the other one was hard of hearing. We all shouted for about ten minutes before Jugs and me broke up laughing. It turns out we was the ones might as well have been deaf, because the girls didn't talk to us ever again. But Jugs had him a great story.

One of my problems was that being from a all-boy family, I didn't have much contact with girls. Mothers is mothers and don't count. The only girl I knew and talked to regular was Dixie Palmer. Dixie lived two houses down in a two-story. Her daddy was a chiropractor, which is the best job you can have in the oil patch. Her and me had known each other since we was old enough to drool. She was in my grade, a year behind Jugs and two in front of Jude. We was good friends, considering she was a girl and couldn't actually play ball with us. Even so, she knew more about baseball than most men. Her daddy was a big Browns fan, and we listened to all the games with him on his big old push-button radio.

Dixie kept the box score at our high school games. After I'd pitch, she'd come over and we'd go through the game a batter at a time and talk about my pitching, whether it was good or bad, and what I ought to thow the batters next time. She was good at planning things out. She always had a plan for everything.

As we got older, I got the idea she wasn't coming over to talk baseball with me as much as she was to be next to Jugs. Jugs, on the other hand, didn't care about talking baseball much after we'd got into high school. He liked to talk about cars and girls and airplanes. Anything fast. I couldn't tell whether he noticed Dixie too much or not.

The night Jugs announced to the family he was joining the Navy to become a naval aviator, Paw got mad, saying he had planned on Jugs working at the furniture store and eventually leaving the store to us boys. Maw cried. Jude cried. I was sad, but I understood wanting to get out of Smackover and wanting to fly airplanes. The getting-out part was every boy in Smackover's goal, except maybe Jude's. Not even Jugs could've made working at the family furniture store fun. If Jugs had had to work in that furniture store for the rest of his life, he'd have withered faster than a Indian on a reservation.

The next morning, Paw drove Jugs to Camden. When he come back that night, he told us Jugs was all signed up and wouldn't be back till he got leave after basic training. Later that night, I went to Dixie's to listen to the game with her and her daddy. I told them about Jugs joining up, and Dixie started to cry. Truth to tell, it was all I could do to keep from crying myself.

3

I got into the majors because of my gooseball. It come from a little game Jugs and me played in the pipeyard.

The pipeyard, over between the ball field and the water tower, was full of racks and racks of oilfield pipe. For something to do between rat killings, Jugs and me took to thowing the ball through the pipes. The straighter and harder you thowed it, the more likely it was to shoot out the other side. The biggest pipe was twenty-four inch by thirty foot long or so. If you thowed hard overhand through a piece in the stack around head-high, you could come within four or five feet of it going all the way straight through. For the longest time, it seemed like no matter how hard we tried, we couldn't thow a ball through without bonging sides or bottom.

Then, one time, I was standing on the other side of the piperack waiting for Jugs to let fly through one of the head-high pipes. I seen him wind up and thow, but I never seen the ball coming. It hit me smack in the groan area. For a joke, Jugs had thowed it sidearm through one of the lower pipes.

From then on, the game took itself a new twist. You couldn't never count on which pipe the ball was coming through. I was forever trying to rack my brother to get even. If I thowed almost underhanded and kept my elbow by my side and flicked my wrist like I would with a curve, I could come pert near thowing that ball straight through the pipe. And if the ball didn't bong the sides of the pipe, there was no way to know it was coming. I never did get even with Jugs, but I did learn me a new pitch—the "gooseball," we called it.

Jugs swore it broke upwards. If it didn't, it sure looked like it done. There's been a plenty of newspaper stories with major league managers saying it didn't break at all—wasn't nothing but a optical illusion. Frankly, it didn't make me no difference whether it broke up or not. So long as the batters couldn't hit it, somebody was going to pay me to thow it.

I was glad to have the gooseball in my arsenal, but the players on the other side started saying I wasn't nothing but a junkball pitcher. This did get under my skin. I had a good enough fastball, a curve that when I thowed it right dropped off the table, and a semi-knuckleball that was getting better but was still prone to hit high on the back-stop.

I started thowing the gooseball as a junior. A course, Jugs was catching me. It was amazing how much better that pitch made me, but Jugs knew better than to have me thow it too much. The next season, the spring of '40, I had a new catcher, Bubba, and he started calling for it more and more.

So as not to telegraph my gooseball, Coach had me to start thowing everything sidearm. Junkball or no, they couldn't hit me, and I went twelve and oh that year with a ERA somewheres near one.

There was even a scout from the St. Louis organization come by that spring. I don't know if he was there to see me or just looking, but Coach told me he said I had "potential." Coach said one of his questions was about my head. Could be he'd heard about the boner I pulled in Little Rock the year before, or could be I just looked dumb on the mound, what with my head being shaped like a potato. Coach told him I wasn't no rocket scientist, but that if I'd keep from daydreaming, I could do all right.

Before that, I never knew Coach thought I was daydreaming. I don't believe I was. It was more concentrating. From as far back as I can remember, when I pitched, I didn't know the score, the day of the week, nor even what month it was. All I thought about was putting the next pitch where Jugs told me to. Jugs did my on-the-field thinking—he told me which base to back up and where to thow on a bunt. Might be I let Jugs do too much of my thinking for me when I was coming up. Maybe if I had of learned early on about making my own decisions, I wouldn't be here today.

I'm glad Coach told me both the good and bad, because it got me excited and working harder, and I especially tried not to think about nothing but pitching while I was pitching. But it was tough and I missed Jugs a awful lot. So did Dixie.

Our senior year, I seen a lot of Dixie. She hung around me mostly to keep up with Jugs. That was okay with me. Everbody in town missed old Jugs.

The snapshots he sent us from all over didn't let us down. Leastwise they didn't let me or Paw down. They was usually of him and his buddies, maybe with their heads stuck through a cardboard muscleman cutout, or them standing under a palm tree with the lowest, flattest horizon you ever seen stretching across behind. Them little square pictures sure enough told us how much fun he was having flying and cruising around the Pacific Ocean on a aircraft carrier.

That spring, it was nineteen and forty, I asked Dixie to go to the prom. We double-dated, and after it was over, the couple we was with made a beeline for the lake to watch the submarine races. A course, neither Dixie nor me was the least bit interested in being romantic. After five minutes of parking, we got to giggling so hard the couple in the front seat got mad and brung us home.

We stayed up a couple of hours then, writing Jugs a letter about what all had gone on that night, which Dixie made sure to say was nothing. Jugs had taken Dixie to the prom the year before, and by some of the things she wrote, I got the idea they might've been a little friendlier than what they had let on. It didn't matter to me. Their business was their business, and the prom to me was just a night that I wasn't pitching nor listening to baseball.

That was also the summer Paw moved out on us. He fixed up a room at the furniture store and stayed there. Him and Maw wasn't never what you'd call romantic, but I had no idea he was going to move out. I asked Maw, and she wouldn't talk about it. Her and Jude both would cry just any minute for any little thing. I spent most of my time gone.

I worked at the store some that summer and saw Paw pert near everyday. He never said nothing and I never asked him nothing. Later I found out he had taken up with a woman from El Dorado. Her name was Lilly, and she was younger and prettier than Maw. She had a figure, too. Maw's big as the side of a house, bless her heart. Lilly used to come by the store, and Paw would act like a kid. He'd crack jokes and shadowbox with me, and do other stuff I never seen him do before. He even smelled different.

Maw sat Jude and me down one day and told us that this woman was a "woman of the night" who had weaved a evil spell over our poor father. She said eventually the spell would wear off, and our father would try to come back, but she hated him so much she would *never* let him set foot in the house again. She also hoped Jude and me and Jugs would hate him, too, after all he had done to us.

Jude told Maw right off that he sure did hate Paw, too, and he'd kill him if he ever tried to get in the house. She smiled. I didn't say nothing. I didn't hate him. Maybe I was supposed to, but he never done nothing to me. I wasn't sorry that he moved out, neither. Not that I didn't like him, but it did make things a good bit more peaceful in the house.

I guess Paw was still keeping us, because we wasn't wanting for nothing that I could tell. Maw knew how I felt, and I believe it aggravated her spite. I couldn't tell from his letters what Jugs knew about it or thought about it. Instead of writing the whole family, he begun to write Maw and me separate. He would tell me just to hang in, and in another year, I'd be signing a pro contract. He'd tell Maw what a good mother she was and how things would work out for the best. Or that's what she said he said. I don't know if he wrote Paw, but I doubt he would've said nothing bad to him, neither.

In June, Dixie went off to college summer school at Fayetteville. I knew she was going on a Sunday night, and I don't know why, but I made it a point not to tell her goodbye. She even come by to see me on her way out of town, and I sneaked out the back door. I reckon I was mad at her for leaving me. I was mad at Jugs for leaving me, too, though I knew deep down they couldn't have done nothing else. I wished I had somewhere to go. I would have been right behind them.

Even with all them distractions, I just kept thowing better and better. Like I said, when I pitched, I didn't think of nothing but. They still couldn't hit my gooseball, and I thowed a perfect game in the summer league that got my picture in the paper here in Little Rock, though they spelled my name wrong. Spelled it *Fiedler.*

I could tell I was getting the big head again on the inside, but on the outside, I'd tell people how I wasn't that good, just lucky. Shoot, I said, I am plumb flattered just to have a couple of major league scouts even *looking* at me. A course, what they was doing was fighting over me. Around town, all of the grown folks would stop me on the street and ask me when was I going to sign a pro contract. Though by now I figured I *was* going to sign one, I'd always play it down to the homefolks. I was the talk of Smackover that summer of '40.

4

It was about half past three in the morning one hot July night when I woke up out of a dream where I was thowing gooseballs to Joltin' Joe, and he was missing every one. I'll never forget, he was just shaking his noggin at them magical pitches I was winging past him.

What woke me up was two people jumping square in the small of my back and then tickling me. Maw come in with Jude trailing behind, and finally got the light on. It was Jugs and Dixie. Jugs was in his dress whites and grinning from ear to ear. Dixie looked like a grown woman. She was beautiful. I hadn't never seen her without what Jugs called her Chinese ponytail—pulled back so tight her eyes slanted. Dixie right off stuck her fist up to Maw's face, and I first thought she'd hurt herself wrestling in the bed. I was laying there in my underwear, trying to focus on Dixie and Jugs dancing around, when finally it hit me. They had got married. To each other.

I can't tell you how I felt exactly, except that my ears started ringing and I got real hot. I remember looking at Jugs and trying to smile and knowing I wasn't doing too good a job of it. Maw started crying—she was probably happy. A course, that set Jude to bawling, though I don't think he had even woke up yet before he started. It was like a reflex with him. Pavlov's weenie is what Jugs called him. That's psychology.

Jugs had come in on leave, and they had got married that morning at the campus chapel in Fayetteville. Jugs told Maw he did it that way to be romantic, but told me later he *had* to do it that way. He knew he couldn't invite Maw without inviting Paw, and he knew Maw wouldn't come if Paw was going to be there. That night, Maw asked Jugs not to tell Paw the good news because it would serve him right for not being at home where he belonged. Jugs told Paw anyway, though.

Maw fixed everbody a big breakfast as the sun was coming up. Jugs and Dixie left early that morning for San Diego by sleeper on what was going to pass as their honeymoon. Jugs's flattop, the *USS Enterprise,* was due to leave on another three-month tour in ten days. I went back to bed about morngloam. I fell to sleep hoping that when I woke up I'd find the business with Jugs and Dixie was a dream, and my dream about Joe DiMaggio was the truth.

Dixie come back from her honeymoon alone and lonely. She said she was moving home from school for good till Jugs got out of the service. With a war tearing up Europe, we all figured it might be a while before he did. We took comfort in him being in the Pacific and not the Atlantic.

Dixie come to some of my games that summer, and I went over to her house to listen to the Browns' games. Her Dad was kind of different towards me since she got married. I reckon he had saved up a bunch of money thinking she would graduate college, and he was sort of mad at Jugs that she quit school before she even finished one term. Or maybe he just got tired of having a potato-shaped head in front of his radio night after night. I don't know.

I know I didn't know how to act towards her no more. She wasn't the girl next door. She was my brother's wife, my sister-in-law. She didn't look the same, neither, and I caught myself looking different at her. I don't think it bothered her like it did me. She was happy as a tick on a speckled pup's ear, and all the time making plans for the future.

That was the summer Jude turned sixteen, and for his birthday, he talked Paw into thowing him a backyard barbecue. He might of hated Paw, but he knew who did the best ribs in Smackover. For the big occasion, Maw let Paw come in the yard, but he could not set foot in the house nor touch her car. Them was the rules.

Jude had asked over a bunch of his egghead friends and their dates. His friends come mostly from the debate team and slide-rule crowd, and I'm pretty sure where they got their dates was from some sort of eyeglasses co-op.

I had promised Paw I'd help him with the cooking. The barbecue pit was set up in the sun, but most of the debating slide-rulers stayed in the carport trying to beat the heat.

To get the fire started, Paw put about a gallon of gasoline on the coals. After the initial explosion, the fire went out. Paw, like he had good sense, picked up the five-gallon gas can, with about four gallons left in it, and begun shaking it on the coals. All of a sudden, the fire flashed, and the flames zipped up from the coals along the stream of gasoline into the nozzle of the can he was holding. The can made a noise like somebody kicked it, and he slung it across the yard. I reckon Paw thought he was on fire, because he fell on the ground and commenced to rolling around and screaming for us to put him out. He might have been a little warm, but he wasn't on fire. The gas can wasn't on fire. Shoot, the *coals* wasn't even on fire. Everbody just watched him roll around and went on back to drinking their lemonade.

That ought to have been enough entertainment for one barbecue, but when the conversation died down a little, Jude felt the need to show out, I reckon. He went in and put on his beekeeper's outfit and got to fooling with his beehive. Couldn't get enough of them slide-ruling debaters to come out to the hive, so he got him a big old clump of bees and brung them to the carport. I figured whatever was going to happen wouldn't be too good, so I went in the house and turned on the baseball game. Seems like I must have locked the back door on the way inside.

I hadn't been in a minute before they was a lot of squealing and screaming from the carport. First the gals, then the fellows, then Paw. I knew what'd happened even before I ever seen the dog fly by the window at a flat-out run. Three or four bodies hit the back door, and I could hear 'em scrambling at the knob. Later, Paw told me that when Jude dropped that gob of bees right in amongst them, he said don't worry, these bees is honeybees and they won't sting. He got that wrong, too.

By Monday morning, Paw was swole up something fierce and sore as a boil. He went to the doctor, and they put him in the hospital in El Dorado. By Friday, Paw still wasn't back at work, and Maw told me to drive to El

Dorado and check up on him. She said if he was really in the hospital and not with that hussy, he oughtn't to be there without his family, and she couldn't go see him because of what he done to her. Jude wouldn't go with me. Said he still hated him for what he done to Maw. I'm sure Jude not wanting to see Paw had nothing to do with how he used Paw for his birthday and then put him in the hospital with his dern no-sting bees. Not that I'd of wanted Jude to come with me anyhow.

When I got to the hospital in El Dorado, they pointed me to the ward where Paw was. He was sleeping. Lilly was sitting in a chair next to his bed. Looked like she had been sitting there all week. When she looked up and seen me, I could tell from her eyes we was talking about more than just some bad honeybee stings. She taken me out in the hall and said how sorry she was, and told me the doctor had found cancer in his liver. The doctor said he probably wouldn't live too long.

Lilly was mighty nice to me. I could tell by what she said—partly by how she said it and partly by how she looked at him—that her and Paw was sure enough attached to each other.

The doctor had decided it would be best if Paw didn't know about the cancer. When he woke up and visited, he laughed about the bee stings and what a mistake it was to have made Jude that beehive and how he was looking forward to the bees' sweet honey anyway. I looked all in his eyes, trying to see if he knew anything. If he even suspected. Only thing I could tell for sure was that his eyes was yellow with the jaunders.

The doctors had told him he'd be leaving soon as he got his strength back, and he told me that'd be in a couple of more days, was all.

I drove on back to Smackover that night in a daze. I wasn't sure what I was going to tell Maw. I was tired when I got home, and I guess mad at her for making me do what I thought she should've been doing, so I just come right out and told her straight. Well, she took it a lot worse than I had ever thought she would. Jude and me tried our dangdest to talk her out of us carrying her to El Dorado that night to be with him. She changed her mind right quick when I finally told her Lilly was at the hospital. After that, Maw said she wouldn't go see him if the doctors said it was the *only* thing that could bring him back from the yawning jaws of death. Jude said he wouldn't go see him, neither, and he hoped he died. Maw said he shouldn't say such of a thing about his father. I went to bed.

5

The next morning, Maw come into my room while I was getting dressed. She said what with Jugs off in the Pacific and Paw fixing to die soon, I was now the man of the house. This little talk went on till it finally got past the bunk and to the point. The point was that I was going to go stay with my cousins in El Dorado for the rest of the summer so's I could sit with Paw every day till he passed. She explained to me how the worst thing in the world is for somebody to die in the hospital without nobody from his family there. She couldn't go, and Jude wouldn't go, so it was up to me.

Now, all I had wanted since I was about four years old was to play major league ball, and to have to quit with two weeks left in the summer season of my last year of high school ball... I talked to Coach, and I believe he felt as bad as me. We was in the running for district, and with me thowing top form, we had a good chance to go to the state finals again—and *this* time, maybe win. But it just wasn't to be. I put some clothes in a paper sack and went to El Dorado. I didn't take neither glove nor ball.

About two weeks after I got down there, I was in the hospital one afternoon, and Dixie and her mother come by to visit. They brung word of Maw and the team and Jugs. It sure was good to see them, especially Dixie. In a way, they seemed more my family than my family did.

They had wired Jugs's commanding officer on the aircraft carrier, and he had promised to try to get him home during this here family crisis—but, then, he *had* just been home to get married the month before.

Paw was wasting away. He had been a nice size man a month before. By now, he had fell off to about a hundred and twenty pounds, and his skin had got yellow like his eyes and was heading toward a kind of orangy-clear color. All he done mostly was sleep. When he talked, he didn't make too much sense. Sometimes he would get to hurting and I'd have to fetch the nurse. They'd give him a shot of something would put him to sleep pretty fast, but even sleeping, he was hurting. You could tell.

One night Paw woke up in a start out of a dead sleep. He begun hollering my name, and when I got up to him he grabbed me around the collar and pulled my face down to his. "Jackson! Jackson! The doctors are letting me die. They quit giving me the medicine. Go get the doctor! Go get the medicine! You got to save me!"

He scared me so bad, I didn't know what to do. I run down to the nurse's station and told them Paw needed a doctor. They said wouldn't none be in till the next morning. I run back to Paw and lied bigger than life about how he was getting better and how he would be coming home in a couple of days and how I wanted to work in the store full-time and eventually be partners with him. I looked into his awful-color eyes trying to tell whether he believed me or not, and I couldn't. To this day, I just don't know.

Lilly was good to me during Paw's stay. She would come by the hospital every evening when she got off work to see how we was doing. Some nights, she'd tell me she would stay with Paw, and she'd give me money to go to the picture show. She was always sweet to be around even though we was in the hospital. I could see why Paw took a liking to her.

The last week or so Paw was alive, he seemed kindly far away. When he was awake, he would look and look at you. You would talk to him, but you couldn't tell what was going on in his head. Once in a while he'd say something, but you got the feeling he wasn't hearing what you said back. He talked a lot about his store. And about Lilly. He talked a lot about Jugs. All the time I was there, he never mentioned Maw.

Jude come to the hospital about four days before Paw died. He wouldn't come in the ward. He got a nurse to come get me out. First thing, he asks whether the prostitute is there. Little priss wouldn't even say whore, let alone call her by her right name. I started to box his ears right there in the hospital, but for some reason I just couldn't get too excited about nothing. I was eighteen years old, and I felt like life had already passed me by.

Jude had brung some papers Maw had got a lawyer to draw up for Paw to sign. I think it was to deed all of his property over to her before he died. They hadn't never got a divorce. Jude explained to me that it was easier to do it now than to have it in a will. Right. The real reason they done it was in case Paw was thinking about leaving anything to Lilly. To get rid of Jude, I told him I'd get Paw to sign. Jude wanted to wait, but I told him to go on home and I'd mail the papers to Maw. I never did ask Paw to sign 'em. I figured it wasn't nobody's business but his. Plus, it's always easier to do nothing.

Paw died August the nineteenth, nineteen and forty, seven days before his fiftieth birthday. He died in the night all by his lonesome with nobody with him. Twenty-nine days I had sat with him from early in the morning till ten in the evening, and he died in the middle of the night with nobody there.

The same day, Smackover lost in the third round of the state playoffs. I read about it in the El Dorado papers just like you'd read about some National League team you didn't care nothing for.

My aunt called Maw and give her the news. She told me Maw said I was supposed to go on back to Smackover to make Paw's funeral arrangements. I didn't know nothing about funerals, much less about making arrangements for them. I'd lived to the ripe old age of eighteen without ever having gone to a real funeral. I'd always played sick or volunteered to babysit to keep from having to go. I told folks I didn't go because it was sick to have the dead body there for everybody to see. "Funerals is a barbarian custom," I used to say. The one I myself had thowed for a cat was for sure.

I was about eleven years old and playing in the cane patch behind our house when I heard a kitten meowing. It took a while to find it. When I did, what I saw made my blood run cold. It was a little bitty kitten without no fur to speak of. It had hair every now and again, but mostly it was just pinkish hide. Just skin covering bones. It kindly scared me.

Now, I loved every animal except rats and razor-backs, and I was glad of the chance to nurse a kitten back to good health, but I was feeling a little careful about picking this one up—not barehanded, anyway. It just kept crawling and squawling, its eyes closed, hoping, I reckon, to find something to eat.

Well, I run back to the house and got a cigar box I used to keep my baseball cards in. I went back to the cane patch, and using the box lid, scooped the little cat into the box without touching it. I taken it back to my room, and put it a washrag in the box for a bed. Then I went in the kitchen and poured it a saucer of milk. Using the washrag so I wouldn't have to touch it too much, I tried to get it to drink. I put its mouth in the milk up to its nose, but it just kept squawling. It acted like it didn't know how to drink. I sure didn't know what to do. I looked it over best I could.

Its eyes was mostly closed, but it looked like just the whites was showing. Real gently, I lifted its eyelids up. It was maggots. Crawling all in its eye sockets. I almost thowed up on my bed.

I took that pitiful kitten out into the woods and buried it in the cigar box. I went back to my room. Even though I never touched it, I washed my hands five times. I couldn't stop thinking about it. Maybe I ought to have killed it before I buried it.

I went back and dug it up. While I was digging, I could hear it squawling still. My stomach was flipping and jumping. I lifted the box out of the hole with my shovel, and tossed it on the ground. The kitten fell out. I whomped that little cat about fifty times with the shovel, hard as I could, all the time screaming at the top of my lungs. I buried it again, this time without the box. I smashed it with the shovel, too, after the kitten.

So, anyway, the undertaker showed me a bunch of coffins, and I picked one with insides that looked like the green cloth on a pool table. I liked pool and thought the tables was distinguished. The undertaker said for laying Paw out I needed to buy a pinchback suit or else go fetch a nice one of his. I went up to the funiture store and looked all around Paw's room and couldn't find nary a suit. I didn't know what to do. He didn't generally wear a suit coat at work. I thought maybe he'd of had one to wear when he took Lilly out.

Lilly! I had forgot to tell Lilly that Paw had died. I hurried to the phone and called her long distance at the bank where she worked. I let her know. She didn't cry. I'll always be thankful I done that and didn't let it slip by like I generally done things. Right before I hung up, I mentioned about Paw's suit and she said if I'd drive back to El Dorado, she would have what I needed. I reckon she couldn't talk out loud there in the bank and I didn't want to make her feel no worse than I figured she done already.

I headed back to El Dorado to see Lilly. When she come to the door of her apartment, she looked like she had been crying. There was some other women inside that I figured was there to comfort her. This surprised me a little bit. I thought she would have kept things a secret.

She told me how sorry she was for me and my family and asked me to come in. I felt funny, and just told her I would take the clothes because I had to get back as soon as I could. I really wanted to tell her thank-you for all she done, but I didn't. I left with a trunk of Paw's clothes in the back seat of his car. She also give me a box of phonograph records she said was his. I never knew Paw to listen to music.

Back in Smackover, I give the undertaker Paw's suit. It was one he must have just bought recently, and it was very snappy looking.

When I finally got home, there was all kind of neighbors and relatives at the house. Even though Paw hadn't lived at the house all summer, and Maw had told anybody who'd listen how she hated him, they hadn't never got them a official divorce. I reckon Maw was still legally a widow and had a right to be in mourning.

She had also been crying, and when I come in, she hugged and kissed me and said what a terrible thing this was and how God had punished our father for what he had done to our family. She asked me had I gotten the legal papers signed, and when I told her no, she hit the ceiling.

My first real funeral was a disaster, front to end. My last funeral surely can't be no worse. As soon as Maw saw Paw in the coffin, she come after me, madder than a stepped-on snake. She wanted to know how come I picked out that zoot suit. She said Paw looked like a dancehall romeo. She said it was a plain down disgrace. I didn't say nothing. I didn't even go look at him. Never did.

At the church, right before the service started, I seen everybody shuffling around and I heard my Maw hollering. Lilly and some of her kinfolks had drove up from El Dorado to pay their last respects. Maw come and told me that since I was head of the family now, I would have to keep that loose woman and her no-account family out of the church. She said it was either the floozy or her was going to be the widow, and if she stayed, Maw was leaving. I just stood there a minute, and the preacher pulled me

aside and said I had to do what my Maw wanted. He said
I was the man of the house now, too. Hadn't nobody ever
once asked me if I wanted the job.

I didn't know what I was going to say to Lilly.

Before I could get to her, Jude run out on the church
lawn and started mouthing off at Lilly and her family,
making them feel less welcome than a briarpatch child at
a reunion. Lilly seen me standing in the doorway of the
church. I could tell she wasn't even hearing Jude, she was
just looking at me. I walked out of the church and told
Jude, who was still screaming cuss words at her, that he
better stop before I stopped him.

She grabbed my hands and looked into my eyes. Hers
was full of water.

"Jackson," she said, "if you want us to go, we'll go."

I said, "No hard feelings Lilly, but I reckon it would
be best. Maw's awful mad."

She said, "I just want to know one thing. Do you hate
me?"

I said, "A course not, Lilly. I don't hate you." And I
didn't.

Lilly got back in her car, and her and her family drove
back to El Dorado, I reckon. I never seen nor heard of her
since.

As I turned to walk back to the church, I saw Jude
giving Lilly's caravan the finger. All my relatives patted
me on the back and told me what a man I was for thowing
that woman out. What a man.

Like I said, I never saw what my Paw looked like laid
out. Everybody said he looked real fine—except, a course,
Maw—but I couldn't bring myself to look at him. Now I
wish I had of. To this day, I get nightmares that he's still

alive in the hospital wanting to know why I quit coming to see him. Now I know why they have funerals and wakes.

6

That fall of '40, I figured my life was a done deal. Uncle Woodley, a shoe salesman from Shreveport, had moved to Smackover and gone into partners with Maw on the store. He took me on full-time and told me I could work there as long as I wanted to.

I reckon I could have got a grant-in-aid to play ball at Arkansas or LSU or somewheres like that. There was lots of talk. I should've took the chance looking back on it, but as usual, I chickened out. Told myself I wasn't smart enough to go to college, which could've been true, but I at least should've been smart enough to try. Plus, I told myself I didn't want college to mess up my pro career, which was a sure enough whopper, because I didn't have no pro career. To make my decision official, I relied on the Bible, which I had learned at a early age to use to my advantage. "After all," I would tell folks when they asked me about going to college, "Jesus only went to school for three days hisself." Really, I wouldn't try for fear of failing. Simple as that.

None of the boys from school had went to college. Quite a few joined the service. Funny, now I remember people talking that fall about maybe us getting into the war. Back then, though, I was so worried about my own self, I didn't pay it much notice.

Jugs was probably worried regular about a war, him being out yonder in the Pacific on the carrier *Enterprise*. The service got him home about a week after Paw's funeral. When he finally did come, things was not the same between us. We was probably both more serious what with Paw passing away and all, and a course, he had a wife now. He didn't even sleep at our house no more. He slept at Dixie's house and spent most of his time with her and her family.

He only got to stay two days. I drove him and Dixie to the bus station the night he left. We all tried to laugh and joke but it wasn't no use. I got the feeling we was all thinking pretty near the same thing. Dixie cried on the way home and I didn't talk. Didn't say a thing to her. I wanted to be anywheres but where I was.

Just before Christmas, Coach come into the store looking for me. After about five minutes of "How's your mama doing?" and "What do you hear from Jugs?" he mentions that a scout for the St. Louis organization had telephoned him and asked about me. He seen me pitch earlier that summer a few times, and agreed with Coach that I had "potential." I couldn't believe it. I figured with me not finishing the last of the season, I was a has-been— or worse, a never-was. I kept Coach in the store for forty-five minutes asking him about everything the scout had said and what Coach thought he meant when he said it. It wasn't much, but it was enough to get me off my backside and amongst the living again.

Coach give me a key to the gym so I could thow after work and on weekends. I could usually Tom Sawyer one of the high school players into thowing with me by telling 'em how I was waiting for a call from the Browns organization as to when to report to camp. Somehow, I don't know how exactly, they also got the idea that once I was playing in the big leagues, I would make sure the Browns' scouts made Smackover a regular stop. When I couldn't talk nobody into catching, I'd thow a rubber ball against the gym wall. My arm was feeling good and boneless.

It was a Friday in the middle of February when I got another call from Coach. He said to come over to the gym quick, that there was someone there to meet with me. This was it. The most momentous occasion of my life.

I run all the way to the gym and probably would have died on the way if I hadn't remembered to breathe about halfway there. I busted through the door of Coach's office and pert near scared the old scout about half to death. I expect I probably looked like a escaped lunatic. Soon as I caught my breath, we got down to business.

I'm mighty glad Coach was there to look after my interest. I was ready to give the Browns all the money I could borrow just for a tryout, but Coach actually got them to agree to pay me, and on top of that, they give me a nice size check and a autographed St. Louis Browns baseball just for signing. When that scout handed me my copy of that signed contract, I was so happy I wanted to climb the water tower and tell all Arkansas.

I didn't. I run home and showed Maw first thing. Who I really wanted to tell was Jugs. Maw seemed to be glad— Jude, too—but I had the feeling neither one of them knew how big a deal this was. Not just for me, but for them, and for Smackover.

I sure enough knew who would appreciate it, though. I run over to Dixie's house and strolled in just like it was another day in Hicksville. After we chewed the fat a while, I handed Dixie the contract. "By the way," I said, "you might be interested in reading this." Well, it took about five seconds before she started hollering and her mother started hollering and her daddy started pumping my hand and pounding me on the back and then we all started buck-and-winging. Dixie's mama broke out the bel-lywashers, and we had a high old time. We all sat around and talked about how it was going to be with me pitching in the majors and how I was going to be the toast of Smackover and how Smackover would have something neither El Dorado nor Camden never had, that being a big-time, major league ballplayer. Dixie's daddy was so excited, he asked me if I wanted a free spinal adjustment. I didn't take him up on it then, but there's been many a time since I was scrunched up in that little pipe in Japan I wished I had taken a raincheck. We talked till late that night and never got tired. I don't believe I had had me a finer day since way before Jugs left.

Things sure was better after I signed that contract. Dixie said I was finally tolerable to be around. I begun spending more time at her house than at my own. I worried a little about wearing out my welcome, but the Palmers, they was nice people and didn't seem to mind.

Ain't it funny? Old scrawny, potato-headed, gooseball-chunking Andrew Jackson Fielder become a overnight bigshot around town. Everybody on the street was wishing me luck and telling me how I ought to pitch to this or that well-known ballplayer. I was having me a big time.

Pitchers and catchers and rookies was to report to spring training two weeks before the rest of the players. I was two out of three of them, and the Browns' front office sent me a one-way bus ticket to camp in San Antonio. I was packed three weeks ahead. I put so much neatsfoot oil on my glove, it soaked clean through my pillow and mattress.

The weekend before I was supposed to leave, Dixie got the idea we ought to go on a picnic. We skipped church and drove up to Rosie's Lake, which had been the site of our famous mudball wars when we was kids. Besides enough food to feed the entire St. Louis Browns organization, we took the rubber inflatable life raft Jugs had sent me postage due from the Navy PX in San Diego. It was the kind pilots used when they ditched in the ocean.

The spring day was warm, but the lake water was still might near freezing. I tried wading out in it, and got about up to my toe hairs before I turned back. We decided to go ahead and launch the raft and float out toward the middle of the lake. The raft was made for one naval aviator, and the two of us was kindly jammed up together. I didn't mind. It was relaxing just bobbing along.

After she squirmed through five or six different positions trying to get comfortable, Dixie finally leaned back in my lap with her head on my chest. I had been that close to her a hundred times before, but something was different. I don't believe I had ever paid attention to what her clone smelled like before, but it was wonderful, like gardenias. She was wearing a shirt-thing with no back, and her skin was softer than anything I ever felt before nor since. Though I knew it wasn't right, I tried peering down over her forehead and into the front of her shirt. I was thinking all kind of crazy things about how I must really love her and how she most probably was so terrible lonely being without Jugs that she probably wouldn't mind if I kissed her, us being related and all.

We laid there and floated and floated. She seemed like she was going to sleep, but I was worried she could feel my heart beating fit to bust out of my chest. I had begun running little scenes in my mind where I'd start out touching her on the cheek, or where I'd start out rubbing my hands through her hair, or where I'd start out massaging her neck—and in every one of them little scenes, we ended up kissing like crazy in the bottom of the raft. I tried to think of other things, I really did, but no matter where I started, I ended up with her in the bottom of the raft.

I was leaving in two days, and I might never come back to this hick town. Jugs wouldn't care; he never got mad at nothing. On and on we floated until we was out in the middle of the lake.

My harmones was driving me so crazy, until I couldn't stand it no longer. I grabbed her shoulders, stuck my feet square between her shoulder blades, and did a back dive out of that raft into the lake. The water was so cold my brain was telling my lungs to take a deep breath while I was still underwater. I decided then and there that I was going to stay underwater either until my mind floated out of the gutter or else I drowned.

Well, even if it hadn't of been too cold, it was sure too far to swim back to shore. When I climbed back into the raft, Dixie said I had scared her spitless jumping in the water like that. She'd been sleeping and didn't know whether I had fell out and was drowning or what. All in all, it was a nice enough picnic. It was one time I believe I made the right decision, especially the way things was to work out.

7

All the pitchers, catchers, and rookies arrived at camp on a Sunday night. I was lost as Grant's Bible. There was veteran batteries, players that had been up and down the farm system like ants on a peachtree, and a handful of rookies like me. Rookies was the least welcome. Rookies was after somebody's *job.*

We talked—mostly about women. Baseball run a not-too-close second. After a while, you could tell the best players talked more about women and less about baseball. The worser a player, the more he yapped about how good he was. I just listened.

Everybody had a nickname in camp. They called me Gooseball, a course. I roomed with a fellow from New Orleans name of "Neckless" Womack. Neckless was a catcher, been with St. Louis for about ten years. He had muscles that run from below his ears straight out to the end of his shoulders. He had more hair on his back than a bear cub. We called him Neckless to his face, but behind his back we called him "Big U," the U standing for ugly, which he surely was.

Neckless didn't have too many friends. Story was, he had once taken a monkey as a pet and taught it to play draw poker. They was very happy until one night he shot the monkey, supposedly because the monkey accused him of cheating.

It appeared to me baseball was something Neckless did to pass the time between prank phone calls. He made a couple a dozen a day. My own particular favorite was one where he'd get a woman mad enough so she'd put her husband on the line. The husband would tell Neckless something like he was a no-good coward and if he ever caught him, he'd kill him. Neckless would take him flat up on that challenge, and tell him he drove a cab and would be right over. Then he'd call the cab company, give 'em the address, and ask them would they please send the driver to the door to pick up some bags.

There was no batters in camp for the first two weeks, and I knew this was going to hurt my chances of making the club. The coaches watched my gooseball and seen what it did, but my gooseball is the type of pitch that's easier to watch than to hit. The coaches liked them big boys that could thow smoke. I was so nervous my pitches was wilder than cannonballs at Gettysburg.

Exhibition games started the second week in March. I thowed a couple of innings in relief here and there, but I couldn't tell much about how I was doing. I was getting hit more than I was used to, but it didn't seem to be no more than everbody else.

I was mighty happy when I made the first couple of cuts and got to go with the team on a road trip to Mexico.

We was headed down to Monterrey to play the Boston Bees in the first major league game ever played in Mexico.

Traveling on the train down there was something. Us Browns took up three cars. Rookies slept in the last car, which was the one that swung the most going around curves. And me being the rookiest of the rookies, I had to sleep in the top bunk in the very back of the last car, which was rotating like a flying jenny. Even after the train stopped, my eyeballs rolled around for another hour and a half.

One of the first nights we spent on the train, the older hands held a team meeting to tell us rookies about some sneak that'd been stealing players' shoes when they was asleep. We was to keep watch. Luckily, I drawed the second shift. The fellow who drawed the first watch got hisself in a real knucklebuster over them shoes. Seems the Pullman porter is supposed to take up the shoes at night and shine 'em and bring 'em back before morning. Didn't none of us rookies know no better, and this here rookie on watch, thinking he was going to be the team hero, jumped the porter first time he reached under a curtain for a pair. He pert near got choked to death before the old hands quit laughing and pulled the porter off of him. The porter didn't think it much of a joke. Nobody's shoes got real shiny that trip.

The things I remember most about that trip was how murdersome hot it was and how Neckless made that fool bet which was almost his last. Mr. White, our manager, had said to be careful what we ate, drunk, and kissed below the border or else we would likely take sick. Neckless got to blowing off about his cast-iron stomach he said come from being born and raised in New Orleans. They egged him on till he ended up betting some of the fellows big money he could eat and drink anything and everything in Mexico and wouldn't get sick a lick.

Well, not only did he get sick, he like to died a terrible death. Me being his regular roommate, I had to help him back and forth to the bathroom. I can still see him sitting there shivering and wimpering like a puppy trying to pass a peach pit. Turns out the fellows had took his toothbrush and rubbed it in every smelly crack between San Antone and Monterrey. Neckless lost a hundred dollars and about half that many pounds.

The ballpark in Monterrey was as nice as most major-league parks here in the U.S. of A. The Mexican fans knew their baseball and was friendly to a fault. They seemed like they was cheering more for us than for Boston, but even with the crowd on our side, the Bees swept the three-game series from us. We stunk.

The veterans acted like they couldn't care less. The rookies was the only ones who took the games serious, and we didn't even get to play. Mr. White was a different story. He got so mad after the last game that he wouldn't let us in the clubhouse until we run about a hundred windsprints. The Mexicans stayed up in the stands and cheered us.

Everbody was relieved when we finally got on the train heading back to San Antone, but we didn't even have time to stop sweating good before Mr. White called a team meeting and announced he'd just lined us up another exhibition game. This one was with a Mexican league team in someplace called Nueva Rosita. Said he'd heard they had some fine ballplayers there who would give their right organ for a chance to play in the majors. Said he believed he'd scout them. Said these fellows was hungry and wouldn't lay down and die like we done in Monterrey.

We rode all night and pulled into Nueva Rosita about two the next afternoon. The whole town turned out to meet us at the station, men, women, and children. They was all grinning and hollering, *"Viva San Luís!"* Acted like they was glad to see us.

We had to walk about a mile down a dirt street to get to the field. Pasture is more like it. Or maybe range land. There was plenty enough stands and the right number of bases, but not a whole lot else to show it was a baseball field. The backstop was made out of chicken wire and had so many holes in it, I would not have watched a game from back there without a catcher's mask, chest protector, and cup. There wasn't no outfield fence. Left field kindly sloped off into a rocky holler. In deep center, they was a bombed-out-looking shack with a Burma Shave sign painted on the one good wall. In right field, they was cows. The only grass in the infield was sticking out of the land mines the cows had left.

The Mexican team's equipment made you want to cry, it was so pitiful. The balls they was warming up with was all fuzzy and lopsided. They only had two bats, both taped top to bottom with electric tape. One bat sounded like bamboo whenever anybody hit with it. And their gloves...well, I had rather of tried to catch with one of Maw's potholders. Neckless said this was how the Indians played baseball before Columbus.

Mr. White told me to warm up. I was going to start. Somehow, it wasn't exactly how I dreamed my first major league start would be. But, hey, it was standing room only, the sun was shining, my gooseball was jumping, the cows seemed interested, and I finally had a chance to prove myself.

Us being the visitors, we come to bat first. It didn't take us long to figure out what *"Viva San Luís"* meant. It meant something like "ya'll never going to make it out of here alive." The fix was definitely on. The first pitch the Mexican pitcher thowed bounced in for a called strike one. I swear, I'd rather have spotted them twenty runs and played it fair than get cheated by a hometown ump on every dern call. It got so bad, our fellows begun jumping across the plate trying to hit pitches the umpire was calling strikes. And the worser the call was, the more the crowd cheered. It was three up, three down for us on nine pitches.

I took the mound hoping maybe the strike zone was just a whole lot bigger south of the border, and he'd call 'em for me like he did for the other guy. Didn't take but one pitch to learn better than that. I don't mean to be bragging, but if there has ever been a more perfect pitch, it was thowed by St. Peter hisself. Right down the middle for ball one, outside. I looked over to Mr. White for help. He looked at the cows. It was my game.

I thowed forty straight strikes, but the umpire give ten free passes in a row for seven runs. They had been at bat for half an hour, and not a one had even swung the bat yet. I recalled worrying before the game that their bats and gloves mightn't last the afternoon. The way this ump called the game, their equipment ought to last through the Second Coming.

Now everybody on the team was looking to Mr. White. There was a good chance the bottom half of the first inning would last until the game got called for darkness, and it was still four hours to sundown. But he had this ya'll-got-what-ya'll-deserved-so-don't-be-bother-ing-me look on his face. I know I had learned whatever lesson I was supposed to, but it wasn't doing me no good right then.

After I started out three and aught against the eleventh batter of the inning, Mr. White called time out, and him and Dominguez, our Cuban second baseman, went and had a powwow with the umpire and the Mexican manager. Mr. White got Dominguez to tell them he didn't mind a little home cooking, but he was going to take his team back to the depot unless things got real fair real fast. The deal they agreed to was us supplying the umpire for the even-numbered innings, and them the odd—if we ever got out of the first.

My next pitch was as good as the other forty-three, leastways for the first sixty feet. It was the four hundred after that what looked bad. This Mexican come around late as last night, but he caught my fastball on the fat part of the bat and sent it to deep right, smack into the herd. It caught one of the cows on the short hop and really got her attention. She looked up, seen our right fielder coming full speed after the ball, and decided she was under attack. She took out after him, and if he hadn't of been the fastest man on the team, she'd of stomped him dead before he clumb the backstop. I don't know if the fans was cheering for him or for the cow or for their batter who'd hit a inside-the-range grand slam home run, but they was going crazy. Them bleachers was rocking like a cheap jungle gym.

I finally got out of the inning on a couple of pop-ups, having give up only eleven runs. My major league ERA was now somewheres around ninety-nine. I almost kissed Mr. White when he come told me he was pulling me. But then I bout dropped stone cold dead when he said I was going to umpire. I knew all the rules and knew what a umpire done, which meant I also knew it was going to be very diffcult for me to umpire a game without making a decision of some sort.

The only thing could be worse than pitching your first major league game in Nueva Rosita would be umpiring your first game there. I done both of them equally poor.

I never did decide whether I was going to call the game fair or get even. Never got the chance. The Browns come to bat and was so fed up with getting home-towned that they clobbered everthing even got close to the plate. Down the holler in left, over the Burma Shave sign in center, deep into the herd in right. I don't believe I had to make a call before we had batted around. We was making a game of it after all, but playing fair didn't set too good with the locals, who took to climbing the backstop and rattling the fences.

Looking back, I believe things begun to make the turn from a game to a revolution when I called Tom Henning safe on a bang-bang play at first. On that one, I know I made the right call, but there was ten thousand or so Mexicans seen it different. They went whoa-nelly nuts. They was screaming, ripping up their hats, thowing chickens. Not speaking Mexican myself, I wasn't exactly sure what they was saying, but I could feel hot breath on the back of my neck from twenty feet away, and that was clear enough.

I looked over in the dugout, and Dominguez was crossing hisself so fast I thought he was going to rub the letters off his shirt. I took this as a bad sign: he could understand what they was yelling. The rest of the team was scrambling around packing up equipment. Mr. White was handing out bats. He didn't want to learn us a lesson no more; he just wanted us to live to lose again.

We had two outs on us. Mr. White decided to pinch hit Bobby Bennett, a rookie infielder, for Jody Faust, our veteran first baseman. I guess he figured the fellows in the dugout had a better chance of survival when the war broke out, and he was protecting the players he knew was going to make the team.

Bobby was shaking so bad, it kindly surprised me when he hit the ball—a one-hopper back to the pitcher. The Mexican pitcher fielded the ball clean and thowed it over to first in plenty of time get Bobby, but the thow pulled the first baseman off the bag towards homeplate. Instead of tagging first, he decides it's easier to tag Bobby. Bobby sees the tag coming and stops dead. The first baseman starts chasing him, and Bobby bolts back to homeplate. Pretty soon, they got him in a rundown between home and first.

Now, Neckless used to tell me that with enough time and bananas, a monkey could figure out Shakespeare. Maybe if I'd of had a little more time and a little less noise, I would have remembered the rule that if a baserunner heading to first turns back toward home, he is automatically O-U-T. At that particular moment, I didn't have time nor quiet nor what little good sense I was born with, so when Bobby come racing back home and slud under the catcher's tag, I made the call the best I could. As loud as I could holler and as steady as I could spread my arms, I yelled, "Safe!! Bat again!"

Everthing went dead still for a second or two. First movement I seen was Dominguez come shooting out of the dugout, waving a bat over his head, mumbling gibberish, and sprinting full speed for the concession stand. He didn't wait around for my call to be translated and pass around the crowd.

Me, Bobby, and the rest of the Browns was right behind him and about twenty feet ahead of certain death. Even Neckless, sick as he was, was able to hurdle the concession stand counter. Dominguez had known what he was doing. The stand made a pretty good fort, and by cocking our bats and flashing our cleats, we was able to hold off the lynch mob. The Mexicans only made one real serious charge at us, and that's when Neckless yelled out, "Remember the Alamo!" Didn't need no translation.

Finally, eight *federales* come riding up on horseback and fired some shots into the air to break up the mob. We double-timed it back to the depot, and luckily the train was there waiting for us. Nobody said much until after we crossed the Rio Grande. Nobody said much to me, even then.

By the time we got back from Mexico, I figured I wasn't going to make it. I don't believe I got a fair shake out of the pitching coaches. I will say this, too, though: the old gooseball didn't baffle them major leaguers like it did them boys round Smackover. If you let 'em look at it enough, they'd start knocking the infielders down with it. Connie White said either I had to mix my pitches up a lot more or he was going to take the married men out of the infield when I was thowing. I wasn't used to mixing my own pitches, especially not by myself.

I got the news I expected about the time camp broke up.

Connie White said, "Son, that gooseball of yours does things I've never seen a ball do before, things I didn't think a ball *could* do. You're good, son. But a pitcher can't be just good. He's got to be a *magician.* He's got to have magic, and use it like a weapon.

"You're a nice kid, Goose. I used to be a nice kid, too, back before electricity. Sometimes I wish I'd stayed nice. But nice guys hesitate. They're afraid of making a mistake, or offending somebody. I don't hesitate and I don't look back—right or wrong, I don't. I get paid to make decisions that win pennants: everything from who bats first to when to hit and run. Those are easy compared to who stays up, who goes down, and who goes home.

"I'm sending you down to Toledo, son. You need to decide whether you want to be a nice boy who's a good pitcher, or a mean-eyed magician working that mound. You'll probably have a better life if you stay like you are, but the Browns can't use you."

So I was going to start in the minors with ten thousand other rejects and retreads. I was going to have to work my way up. Fair enough. I went down to the minors with the idea that I'd be back to the Browns in a month or two. Didn't happen quite that way.

A pitching coach down in Toledo told me I needed one more pitch with the four I was thowing. I had a fastball, a change, a curve, and my gooseball. I needed a knuckleball, and I never had mastered that sucker. He also said I had to work on getting my motion the same for every pitch I thowed. Said a batter could tell ever time a gooseball was coming by the way I dipped my shoulder before I let loose of it. I knew he was right. Jugs used to tell me that.

I worked plenty hard that season of '41. They give me a stainless steel baseball to hold in my hand all day long on the days I wasn't pitching. My fingers and wrist got lots stronger. I felt like I was able to thow a little harder a little longer. And I was learning. Everbody was working hard and learning.

Well, almost everbody.

There with the Mudhens, we had us this one fellow who'd caught in the majors two, three years back. Name of Ernie Musso. He was from Brooklyn, in New York City. Since we was all trying to get to the bigs, and since he had been there, he figured he was better than the rest of us—and he wasn't shy about it, neither. Even our *coach* hadn't played in the majors, and Musso was always giving *him* advice and telling the rest of us how ignorant he was when things didn't go right. Old Musso claimed he was just down here in the minors "temporarily" on account of he had got hit in the eye with a fastball. There was two fellows in Toledo had been around at that time, and they told us his teammates had went together and bought the pitcher that hit him a box of Havana cigars.

Once, after we lost both games of a Sunday double-header, he give the entire team a lecture on the make-or-break aspects of waiting for the right pitch. He even talked straight at Coach a time or two, jawing about how important it was to impress upon the younger boys that this was how they would make it "to the majors, like myself"—waiting for the right pitch. We called it the "sermon on the mound."

Normally, one of the bigger guys would have beat Musso to a greasy spot as often as necessary until he quit acting so smart. I ain't altogether sure why they didn't. But Musso kept hinting he was being groomed for a big-league managing position. He talked about going back up as a player "or in some other capacity." He also must have told us six hundred times how he personally knew Mr. Weisman, the Browns' owner.

It was my thinking that the guy was nuts. Looked to me like he talked about coaching partly because he figured he was safe as long as somebody thought there might be some truth to it, and partly because he had begun to believe his own bunkum.

After the "sermon on the mound," some of the guys started talking about poisoning Musso. It *had* been kindly funny with Neckless. But I got a better idea.

We told Coach we needed some Browns' team stationery to play a little joke on Musso. He squinched up his eyes and looked at us a minute before he said, "Sorry, boys, I might be fired if I was to give you some of that team stationery which is in a grey box in the top drawer of that there filing cabinet."

Yessir, that paper even had Mr. Weisman's name on it. We wrote a letter to Musso like it was from him, hisself. We typed it and everything. In it, we had Mr. Weisman carry on about how great a player Musso had been in the majors, and what a leader he was with the youngsters in the minors. The letter ended by saying that he had decided to bring Musso back up to the majors as the St. Louis player-manager, replacing Connie White, that had been the manager of St. Louis since the Civil War. Now, Musso was to keep all this under his hat, but he was to catch the next train and report directly to Weisman at the team office in St. Louis. He was to tell our coach he had a death in the family and would be taking a leave of absence for a week. During that time, "it was hoped" him and Mr. Weisman could come to "a mutually agreeable contractual arrangement."

We backed the letter to Memphis, our next road stop. We put it inside another envelope and sent it to a friend of one of the guys in St. Louis to mail so's it'd have a St. Louis postmark.

At the team meeting before our last game in Memphis, Coach told us Musso had been called away because his grandmama had died. We let out a big hoop-and-holler that scared Coach a little. He said, "What? You goobers didn't have anything to do with Musso's grandmaw's dying, did you?" We told him what we done. He said we shouldn't have done it, and then he laughed as hard as any of the rest of us.

Only bad thing was, we never found out what *exactly* happened when Musso met Mr. Weisman in St. Louis. But he never rejoined the team, and neither did he replace Connie White as manager of the Browns.

That season in the minors went pretty good for me. I started eight games for the Mudhens, and my record was four and one. ERA was under two.

My big break come in the last game of the minor league season. I pitched a no hitter on my nineteenth birthday, August the twenty-seventh, nineteen and forty one. The St. Louis papers picked it up, and so did the Smackover paper and a whole bunch in-between. I used to carry the clipping in my wallet.

Mr. Weisman called me personally and congratulated me. I wanted real bad to ask him about Musso, but I didn't.

8

Two days later, I got a call from the front office saying they was purchasing my contract from Toledo. At first, I thought they was letting me go, what with the minor league season being over and all. Finally, the fellow on the other end noticed I wasn't quite as excited as I ought to been, and he spelled it out for me. Said I was supposed to report to Philadelphia to join the Browns by the end of the week.

Everbody on the Mudhens said they was excited for me. I knew they was all wishing it was them and telling theirselves it should have been. Sometimes you got to lie to yourself to keep yourself going. I learned that in Japan. And really, I knew it was the no hitter that got me the call, pure and simple. Still, I ain't one to look a gift horse in the mouth.

I finally got to the Benjamin Franklin hotel in Philadelphia about two in the morning. Neckless was the only player in his room. He was doing what he could to enjoy the city over the telephone. Come to find out, this is what he always done with his spare time on the road trips. Back in St. Louis, he would go out some—long enough to pull the fire alarm in the visiting team's hotel about three o'clock every morning so they'd have to file out in the street and couldn't get a good night's sleep before the game.

Soon as I got there and said hidy, Neckless told me to go report right away to Mr. White in a room down the hall. It took me a while to get him to answer the door, and when I did, I could tell right away it was a mistake. He was pretty mad at getting woke up. After I explained that Neckless had said I was supposed to, Mr. White got nicer and told me I ought to go right away and introduce myself to all the players. I thought about telling him wasn't nobody in yet, but then I thought twice about it, and just went back to Neckless's room and tried to sleep between prank calls.

Next day at Shibe Park, Connie White told me he'd brung me up as a relief pitcher. I watched the games against the Athletics from the bullpen. Now, don't get me wrong, I was glad to be up in the bigs, and the bullpen was more exciting than the furniture store by a long chalk. But I have to tell you, watching a game from the outfield waiting on the manager to signal for me to come in in a clutch situation about made me a nervous wreck. All of my life until then, I had been the kind that throve on being put in in the toughest pinch. But sitting out in that bullpen, I found myself praying that I wouldn't have to go in and relieve. And I mean, praying *hard*.

I reckon being a relief pitcher might be the world's craziest job. Once the game started, the relievers was sent down to the bullpen, which most times was in a spot that wasn't fit even for cheap seats. You couldn't hardly see the game, so you made up games amongst yourselves. We'd make up teams like the All-Ugly Team, the All-Slob Team, and like that. Spitting tobacco juice on bugs was a favorite competition to them that chewed tobacco. Blowing smoke rings was what smokers done.

I never took to tobacco, chewing nor smoking. With the Mudhens, I had started one game with a big chaw. The leadoff man bunted, and it wasn't until after I thowed him out that I noticed I had swallowed most of it. Like a man once told me about a particular bunny rabbit, "It won't kill you, son, but it'll make you wish you was dead."

Me, I chewed gum. I used to chew about twenty sticks to where it got good and soft. Then I'd stretch it out like taffy so my hands was about eight inches apart. I'd wait for a fly to land and then I'd clap my hands and trap him in the gum. Sometimes I got as many as a hundred flies, depending on how clean they kept the bullpin and how close it was to a hot dog stand. I could catch more flies in a inning than the outfield could catch in a double-header.

In Boston, my time run out. We had tied the game three-three in the eighth, and Connie White had pinch hit for the pitcher. Soon as they announced the pinch hitter, they motioned down for me to start warming up. I was a mess. My hands was shaking. I was feather-legged. I put myself together and thowed a few warmup pitches, and most of them the catcher was able to catch.

Finally, Connie White signaled me to come on in. I started out the bullpin, but another pitcher grabbed me by the belt just long enough to wish me luck and stick a three-foot piece of toilet paper down the back of my pants. I reckon it flapped out behind me like a tail while I trotted through the outfield and onto the mound. Looked like they come got me off the can to pitch to a few batters.

Neckless was catching, and he come out and told me just to keep the ball low and let him do the thinking. He also pulled the toilet-paper tail from out my pants.

The first pitch he called for was a fastball. Jugs had always told me to thow my fastball straight down the middle. That way them looking for a low ball would swing under it and them looking for a high ball would swing over it. I wound up, let fly, and as the ball left my hand, I knew something was terrible wrong. It kept fading to the right, fading to the right, heading smack for the batter's head. He was young and had good reflexes and was able to dive out the way before I give him brain damage. That scared me so bad, I could feel my knees wobbling.

The Red Sox crowd started booing and one fellow in the Boston dugout took to yelling things about Maw, most of which wasn't true. I did my best not to listen to him. A walk, a double play, and a groundout got me through the inning. When I come to the bench, the boys patted me on the back and said I done good brushing back that first batter. Connie White called it a "gutsy move." Neckless said, "Good work, kid. They can't hit lying down." They all enjoyed it so much I didn't have the heart to tell them the ball had just got away from me.

Well, we got a couple of runs in the top of the ninth, and I was able to hold out in the bottom half to get my first major league win. The whole club made a big deal out of it and made me feel real good. In the locker room, they started chanting, "Gooseball! Gooseball!" and took turns popping me with wet towels. I had done arrived. I was due.

I was happy as a pig in sunshine. I went back to the hotel and fell asleep hoping when I woke up, it would all still be true. Seemed to me it might have all been *too* good. Nothing was real after Connie White motioned me to start warming up. I had run it over in my mind a million times ahead of time, so when it was really happening, I *could* of been just daydreaming again. I wondered whether I wasn't going to wake up in my bed in Smackover after another good baseball dream.

Dixie and her daddy called me in the wee hours of the morning to tell me they had listened to the game and had been trying to get through to me all night. Most probably Neckless was beating up taxi drivers by telephone. They was sure enough excited, and said that when I went into the game, the Smackover phone lines was jammed in about two minutes what with everbody calling everbody else to tell them Smackover was on the map. They woke me out of a dead sleep, but got me so fired up talking that I didn't shut my eyes again that night. I was in the Big Leagues. I even had an official nickname. It was printed right there on the front page of the sports section of the Boston paper. The newspapers liked me. The fans liked me. And, helped along by me pulling off some practical jokes, even the other players was starting to like me.

We did have us a high time or two, tricking around. Like with Will McNulty, our left fielder. We called him Feets because he wore a size seventeen cleats, and when he run, that's most of what you seen. We got rained out in Cleveland one time and had nothing to do while we was waiting to play a double-header there the next day. We snuck Feets's shoes out his locker and left another pair in case he happened to be looking in his locker for no reason. Then we painted his cleats pink, both tops and bottoms. After they dried, we blacked 'em again with boot black.

The next day was Sunday, and the outfield was still wet since it hadn't been covered by the tarp. It wasn't until about the third inning, after Feets had run down a couple of extra-base hits, that the pink started to show through the boot black. The fans was wondering why Feets was playing barefoot. He didn't have but one pair of cleats, so he was stuck. When he come to bat in the fifth, the crowd went crazy. He struck out on a bad pitch and he come back to the dugout hunting for the fellows that had embarrassed him so. A course, Feets had grew to fit them big feets, so we all taken a blood oath not to rat on each other, and it ain't been broke to this day. I wouldn't be telling you, Major, but like you said, everything I say in here stays in here.

When we come back to Sportsman's Park in St. Louis for our last home stand, we was right in the home stretch of a pennant race with the Yankees. I couldn't get over the fuss people was making over me and my gooseball. Reporters was all the time hoovering around, asking me to speak a few words so they could make me out either a good guy or a bad guy. That's the way the newspapers work, if you don't already know. If the first things you say to them is good, then they turn you into a good guy. If you say something bad about somebody or thow a tantrum or, Lord help you, don't say nothing at all, they make you out a bad guy. I was careful to say sweet things about everybody, even the umpires, and acted like I didn't deserve all the fuss they was making over me.

And, the truth told, I really didn't. I was just a new face in a six-month-long season. There was columns about Gooseball Fielder nearly ever day of that week-long home stand. I felt bad about them making such a fuss. I felt bad for all the veterans that had brung the team this far. I didn't blame the guys for being a little bit green about all the attention I was getting. I just tried to let them know that it wasn't none of my doing. To make things worse, ever time one of our pitchers walked a batter, the fans started yelling "Gooooseball! Gooooseball!" hoping Connie White would bring me in.

I made four appearances in seven games. Pitched a total of eight innings and didn't give up but one earned run. My ERA was one point thirteen so far. The gooseball wasn't rising like it could, but it was still fooling the batters. I think all the press was helping. Wouldn't nobody have paid me or my gooseball no never-mind if they just seen it now and then when I come in in relief. But the more they read about it in the paper, the more they thought about it. The more they thought about it, the better it worked on 'em. That's psychology.

After I come in and struck out four against Detroit in two innings, they printed a article about the gooseball and whether it was really rising like was claimed. The manager for Detroit said it didn't rise, it just looked like it did. Detroit's cleanup hitter, Big Ben Dampf—remember him?—he said it didn't rise, it just didn't fall as fast as it was supposed to. The Movietone News people come out and filmed it in slow motion and had a Yale professor talk about it being impossible that it had rose. He said it was a optical illusion. But then, he also said a curveball didn't really curve. I remember, after I heard him say that, I wasn't so sorry I hadn't gone to college. Neckless told the reporters I had goosedown in my resin bag, and when I rubbed it on the ball, the ball got lighter. I figure Neckless and the Yale professor cancelled each other out.

I got to admit though, I was on top of the world. Maw called and said her and Jude was keeping a scrapbook on me. Dixie called and told me her and Jugs was expecting a baby in March. They said if it was a boy, they was going to name it Andrew Jackson Fielder II, after me. My old high school coach called and said he was proud one of his boys had made it big. He told me don't try too hard and keep my head in the game. I thanked him for all he had done for me.

The pennant race finally boiled down to the last three games in the season, which happened to be against the Yankees at New York City. We was two games behind, so we had to sweep the series to win the pennant. Though we was square in back of the eight ball, we felt like we could do it if we got some breaks. We'd been hitting real good, and the relief pitching was letting us hold onto leads in the late innings.

We won the first game two-oh, with Buzzard Broderick, our ace right-hander, going all the way. I kindly wanted to come in and show everbody my gooseball could do the job, but I also kindly wanted to stay in the bullpin and not mess up. When I watched a game, I wasn't thinking about nothing but the next pitch and whether it got me closer to going in or not.

Sunday's game was rained out, and they scheduled a double-header for Monday. This meant the pennant was going to be decided in one day in New York, and everbody that could buy or steal a ticket was going to be in the stands for the duration. I was glad the game got rained out because it give one of our starters a extra day's rest, which meant they was one more pitcher could thow instead of me.

I had near about made my mind up once and for all that I didn't want to pitch again ever. I'd settle for the little bit I had done to help the team so far, and hopefully take home that pennant bonus. I didn't want to be no hero. Well, that ain't exactly true. I reckon I feared being the goat more than I wanted the chance of being the hero.

We had a team meeting Sunday night, and Connie White give us a pep talk. He didn't have to say much. It was like pep talking coon dogs before a hunt. No need for it. He also told us to stay away from the booze. He didn't have to worry about that with me. I had decided a long time ago that what I wanted to do was play in the big leagues, and booze wasn't going to get me no further along down that road. Connie White also said for us to stay close to the hotel.

New York was a place you could get into trouble by accident, without even trying. People thick as hops. It was kindly scary to me. Ever since I was a little boy, I'd heard stories about New York City and what a hard town it was. Neckless told me how you was supposed to walk in New York. It's like you could walk anywhere, but ever four or five steps, you had to reach back and put your hand on your wallet to make sure it was still there. Having lived on the road for six months, everthing important I had was in that wallet, including all the money I owned.

That Monday morning of the double-header, I was a bundle of nerves. Tried to eat breakfast, but I couldn't, so I decided to go walking to calm down some. Being stuck inside the day before because of the rain had made me even edgier than I might of been anyhow.

I knew better than to ask Neckless to come. He hated New York more than your average American. Everytime I asked him to go somewhere in New York, he said the same thing: "I wouldn't walk across the street to see the Statue of Liberty thow her paint brush across New York Bay."

The last time I had went somewhere with him in New York, he near about got us arrested. We was eating in a respectable restaurant downtown when some Yankee fans come up and asked him how Buzz Kleinpeter thowed his spitball. They was doing it just to aggravate him, and I figured he'd just tell 'em where to go or something. But no—old Neckless stands up, takes off his jacket, grabs a ashtray off the next table and dumps it out on the carpet, spits in it—and not mouthspit, he hawks this up from the bottom of his gizzard—takes a full windup, and with everbody watching now, he slings the ashtray through the place head-high and it explodes on the back wall. He put his jacket back on, sat down, then asked the Yankee fans, "Did you notice the break?"

I wasn't going to ask Neckless to go along.

I walked and walked till I come to Central Park, and then I walked through there for what must've been a hour or more. It was as pretty a place as I'd ever been in. Like a outfield, but with trees and ponds.

I heard some church bells and asked these old fellows playing checkers what time it was. They said five to twelve, and I nearly fell out. I was supposed to be back at the hotel for noon to ride the bus with the team to Yankee

Stadium for the one-thirty opener. I was going to have to go straight to the stadium.

I thought about taking a taxi, but I hadn't never taken one before. I figured the driver'd play me for a clodhopper and try to take advantage of me. Well, I would outsmart *him*. I would take the subway. After asking a few folks, I got on the right train going to the field. Everbody on the train was talking about the game. I wanted to tell them who I was, but I figured that wouldn't be too smart. Yankee fans ain't famous for their kindness.

The train stopped at the stop I wanted, and me and a couple thousand other folks jumped off. Some fellow bumped me as I was stepping off the train. I didn't think nothing about it for about two steps, and then I reached to slap my wallet and it was gone. I swung back around, and there he was in the door staring at me. I hollered at him and he took a step backwards into the car. The doors was closing. All I could think about was losing everything I had. I reached into the train door just as it was closing and grabbed him by the shirt. I ripped the front of his shirt plumb off and was holding it when the door shut all the way and the train took off. There he was, just staring at me through the window with his mouth hanging open, the dirty crook.

Well, I tell you, not even the chance of winning the pennant could have cheered me up after that. Besides everthing else, that wallet had my four-leaf clover in it that I'd had since I was ten years old, and I wasn't sure exactly how much that clover had to do with me being where I was. I got to the clubhouse on time and went ahead and dressed out. I tried to forget about my wallet, but I just couldn't.

Neckless had missed the team bus, too, and come in the latest, as usual. He sidled up and asked me where I'd been that morning. I didn't feel like talking to him, but he kept on pestering. Finally, he said, "Well, you left this on your dresser." It was my wallet! I was back in business. The world was back on its axle. I stuck my wallet in my street shoes and laid 'em down right next to the piece of plaid shirt that I had snatched off that man on the subway. He probably was a Yankee fan, anyway.

The first game of the double-header was the best baseball game I ever seen or even heard about. The stands was packed and every pitch—ball or strike, swing or miss—got itself good and cheered, or booed, one. New York jumped out to a three-one lead in the first on a walk, a error, and a home run. We come back with another run in the second and two in the third to take the lead. We was playing baseball as she is taught. Get a man on first, get him to second however you can, and pray for a base hit.

In the bottom of the fifth, a two-run homer put the Yanks back in the lead and sent Buzz Kleinpeter, our spitballer, to the showers. Because of the rainout, we was able to send in another starter in relief. We tied it up in the top of the sixth on a picture-perfect squeeze play. There was times in the late innings when both teams looked like they was going to bust it wide open, but something always happened to shut down the rally. Feets stole a home run from their clean-up man in the bottom of the ninth. That sent the game into extra innings and sent our second pitcher packing. Connie White motioned for me and Injun Joe Judson, our left-handed reliever, to start warming up early in the inning.

Things worked out, praise the Lord, so that Injun Joe got called in instead of me, and I sat back down in the bullpin. In the top of the thirteenth, our lead-off batter knocked one into the cheap seats to break the tie, but that's all we could get out of the inning.

We started the bottom of the thirteenth, and Connie White had me and another right hander warming up. The Injun was thowing pretty well but got into trouble and loaded the bases with one out. My knees went to jelly again, but a miracle double play won us the game and saved me from a breakdown.

One more game to go, this one for all the money.

The last game started before we really had a chance to let the first game sink in, but that was probably for the best. There wasn't much talking on the bench. Everybody knew they had a job to do and was ready to do it. Except maybe me. On my way out to the bullpin, Connie White grabbed me and spun me around, looked me square in the eyeballs, and told me to stay ready. I said I would, but the words kindly stuck in my throat on the way out.

This game was different than the first one. We jumped out to a two-oh lead in the second, and that's the way it stood till the ninth. In the bottom of the ninth, New York loaded the bases with one out. The crowd was standing up and yelling at the top of their lungs. I never heard nothing like it. It was so loud that if you didn't shut your mouth hard, it would make your teeth rattle.

Connie White signaled for me to start warming up again. I knew in my mind I was going in there this time. Besides being the last pitcher left in the bullpin, I had sinned enough and read enough scriptures to figure God had set me up for just this moment. I thought about spiking myself, but I chickened out.

Our back-up third baseman, Fuzzy Pastorek, had pinch hit for somebody, I forget who. Why that jackass was allowed inside the basepaths, I do not know. He could hit fair to middling, but he hadn't fielded a grounder clean since Prohibition. I hadn't never seen one hit to him that didn't come back to the pitcher with shoe polish on it. Anyway, he kicked a double-play ball into the outfield and let them Yanks score their first run and load the bases again.

The next batter smacked a line drive to the wall. Feets caught it on the tip of his glove, but the sacrifice let New York score another run and tie up the ballgame. It also sent our pitcher to the showers.

I started making deals with God you wouldn't believe. I pledged my pennant share to the orphans back home, and twenty percent of my next year's salary was going to the church of His choice. But God wasn't dealing that day, and Connie White signaled for me.

Coming in from the bullpen to the mound, I couldn't breathe. I was worried enough about not walking funny that I started walking funny. There was a "OOOOOOOOOOO" from the stands so loud it made me feel like I was going to pass out. In St. Louis, that sound meant that they was saying "Gooooose," short for gooseball. In New York, it sounded more like boos.

When I got to the mound, the whole infield and Connie White was there. They told me I could be nervous as I wanted to, long as I stayed loose and thowed strikes. They looked worse nervous than me. Connie White handed me the ball. "*Magic,* son," he said. "It's time."

Neckless was the last one to leave the mound. He told me the score was tied; they was men on the corners, including Mudbug McCullough, the fastest white man in America, on third; we had two outs; and the number-six man was up. As he turned and headed to the plate, I started to yell for him to come back, but I figured he couldn't hear me. Not that I had anything to say to him. I just didn't want him to go. I wasn't ready to start things off just yet.

I toed around at the rubber, trying to fix the different holes in the mound the other pitchers had dug during the twenty-something innings played so far that afternoon. The air smelled like the state fair in Little Rock. I think it was a combination of popcorn, peanuts, beer, sweat, sump water, dust, and dying grass.

I had some warm-up pitches coming. I rubbed the ball in my glove like I done a million times before. Kept telling myself it was the same ball, same glove, same field, same rubber, same distance to the plate, and that it wasn't nothing more than a game meant for children. But my hands kept on shaking and my knees kept on knocking and my eyeballs kept on racing around the ballpark, I reckon looking for a place to hide. Even on top of all the noise, I could hear my heart beating in my ears. I remember worrying that I hadn't swallowed nor blinked in a long time.

Since they was men on base, I decided to warm up out of the stretch. I took my stretch, brought the ball back and let her rip. Neckless didn't even get up out of his stance. He just watched the ball fly over his head and hit the backstop about fifteen feet up. The crowd went crazy. Some wiseacre started blowing a goosecall. Neckless come trotting back to the mound and handed me a new ball. He said to take a couple of deep breaths. I tried, but my lungs just would not open up. I glanced over at Connie White. Everbody on the bench was looking at him, too. He was looking up to heaven. I remember wondering how they'd do the box score if I was taken out of the game before I even thowed one official pitch.

I decided I better dance with the one I brung, as the saying goes, so my next warm-up pitch was a gooseball. It broke late but stayed right where I put it. I thowed a couple more warmups and the umpire yelled at us to PLAY BALL. I didn't need but one out. Seemed like a lot.

The batter, Frenchy d'Aquin, you remember him, he stepped into the box and knocked the dirt off his cleats. He slammed his bat down on the plate hard and give me a mean stare. He looked older than Paw and twice as sore. He got up real close to the plate and dipped down so his lead shoulder was almost over the plate. His head was swuvveled around on his neck like a owl. This bothered me. I got the signal for a gooseball from Neckless. I took my stretch, checked the runners at first and third, and let her fly.

I could tell when the ball left my hand something was wrong. I watched that gooseball home in on Frenchy's ear. I seen his eyes get big as hen eggs, and all I could think about was that I was fixing to kill him, but a miracle happened. The ball hit his bat and went foul. Strike one.

Them Yankee fans wasn't too crazy about that. They thought I tried to stick it in his ear on purpose. I wish I had of. Then, at least, I'd have known I had *some* control. As it was, I didn't know why my pitch got away, let alone what I was going to to do to fix it. The crowd had got even crazier. Them was definitely boos.

One thing they tell you in little leagues is not to aim the ball. This is good advice and always has been. What you do is you just concentrate as hard as you can on the catcher's mitt and think the ball into the mitt. I knew what I had to do. I had to thow strikes.

It could of been that the ball slipped off of my fingers, so I stepped down behind the mound and grabbed the resin bag. I come back up concentrating my mind on nothing else but that catcher's mitt.

That's when it happened. I started my windup. That's right. Can you believe it? Shoot, what am I talking about, you probably remember it near about as good as me.

I been playing baseball *all my life,* and me, with the score tied, with a windup slow as a grandfather clock, with Mr. Speed hisself itching to run on third, I take me a windup. Right as I started up, even with the crowd roaring louder than three freight trains and a tornado, I heard the Yankee third base coach telling McCullough to go home. I knew if I didn't speed up my motion, he'd beat the ball home, and I knew if I changed my motion at all, I'd balk him home just the same.

With my left eye on the catcher's mitt and my right eye following McCullough down the basepath, my pea-for-a-brain told my body to speed up my thow, slow down my motion, die, dig a hole and disappear, all at the same time. My body short-circuited, went to gyrating, tied itself in a boy scout knot, and done a bellyflop off the mound. The last thing I seen before my face hit the grass was the ump come shooting out of his squat yelling "*BAAAALLLKK,*" louder than God.

I laid there face down in the grass. It was over: the season, my life. Ruined by a bonehead choke. I kept my eyes shut, hoping maybe Maw would wake me up and I'd be back in Smackover, but I could hear the stampede of fans all around me. After a couple of minutes, a big foot rolled me over on my back. Mudbug McCullough pulled the gameball out of my hand. He said, "Nice dive, Fielder," and then give me the horselaugh.

Somebody come by and swiped my cap right off my head. I didn't even move. Somebody else come by and ripped my shirt. I didn't even care. I figured it might have been the fellow from the subway. The New York fans hoisted me up on their shoulders and carried me around the infield two or three times. I was a hero for the wrong town. After a while, they dumped me back on the mound headfirst. At some point, I stood up, checked my zipper, come down off the mound, and walked through the dugout into the clubhouse.

The other players was looking at me and whispering, but they was nice enough not to say nothing to my face. I had cost them some big money. But I had cost Mr. White the pennant, the one thing him and the Browns had never had but wanted more than life itself. I figured he was sending somebody out to find a shotgun to kill me once and for all, which he would have never been convicted of after what I had pulled.

I thought about just walking on away without changing out of my uniform. I decided not to because it made me a easier target, and it give Mr. White a legal right to shoot me if he didn't already have one. I also decided not to take a shower because my instincts told me it was not a good idea to get naked in front of thirty or so fellows that hate you worse than a bad tooth. I put on my civvies as fast as I could and tried to avoid Mr. White by sneaking out through the dugout.

The field was dark, and I thought I had escaped when I seen a shadow at the far end of the dugout. Mr. White motioned for me to come see him. Before I could even say I was sorry, he said, "Indecision will kill us all, son," and he walked away. I never said nothing.

I didn't go back to the hotel to get the rest of my clothes. I caught a cab to the train station and spent the night there waiting for the next train out to Little Rock. I would have give a war pension to be back in Smackover that night.

The next morning, the headlines in the New York papers was wrote about two feet high. One said "Goofball Chokes, Yankees Steal Pennant." I knew this meant the end of baseball for me. When you ain't got the *head* for baseball, you're through. That ain't nothing nobody can learn you.

9

When I didn't show up for the train home with the team,
all kind of rumors started in the papers about what had
happened to me—or what they hoped had happened to
me. Some of the papers said somebody seen me jump off
the Brooklyn Bridge. A sportswriter wondered if I had
took a windup before I thowed myself off. Somebody else
said a group of loyal St. Louis fans that had made the trip
to the big city had killed me or at least put parts of me in
the hospital. Somebody else reported that me and Ernie
Musso was seen in the company of some New York
Italian-type gangsters sipping champagne after the game.
One reporter even called my mother back in Smackover
to see if she'd heard from me and asked her whether me
losing the game would affect our relationship. I don't
know what she told him. The headline in the *St. Louis
Post-Dispatch* read "Mother Gooseball Hopes Ugly
Duckling On Way Back To Nest."

   I tried to slip back into Smackover but it wasn't no
use. Everbody—man, woman and child—knew me. The
ones that didn't before did now. They had been running

my picture on the front page of every paper in Arkansas. I felt like a milk bucket under a bull.

When I got to the Smackover bus station, the depot manager asked if I'd mind him calling the *Commercial Appeal* in Memphis and telling them I had come home. Said they was worrying him to death about me, and there was twenty bucks in it for him. I told him to go on ahead, and while he was at it, why don't he kick him a few dogs.

Still, I was bound and determined I wasn't going to let nothing nobody said get my dander up, except for Jude, and I decided the first time he opened his mouth, I was going to whomp him like a rat at a rat killing.

For some reason, I just didn't want to go to my house. I decided to head over to Dixie's first and get the latest on Jugs. Dixie was prettier than a cream of soda to a dying dry man even though she was out to there with expecting. Her and her mama and daddy seemed downright glad to see me, too. They wanted to know all about New York City, and they laughed fit to bust when I told them the story about my wallet. They waited for me to start talking about blowing the pennant, and when I did, they said they was proud of me anyway, that it was something could happen to anybody. Even though I knew it was the most boneheadedest play that's probably ever been pulled in sports since the Christians took on the lions, it still made me feel good that they was trying to help.

They wasn't too much news of Jugs. He'd been stationed as a torpedo bomber on the *U.S.S. Enterprise* out of Hawaii. Dixie said he was still pulling her leg regular in his letters, but what with a youngun coming, she was getting more and more worried about him.

New York beat Brooklyn in the series that year in five games. I listened to most of it on the radio at Dixie's house. Before long, it was like I hadn't never left Smackover. Spent the rest of the fall working part-time at the store for my uncle and hoping something would happen to me so I wouldn't have to show back up for spring training in '42.

I don't believe my wishing had anything to do with us getting into the Second World War in December, but it sure give me a fine excuse not to play ball the next year. On the morning of December 8, nineteen and forty-one, I was in the line in front of the El Dorado recruiter's office waiting to join the Army Air Corps. When the recruiting sergeant asked me if I had any nicknames, I said I didn't. It was all right by me to fight for my country and die if I had to, but I didn't never want to play baseball—nor even *talk* about it—ever again.

Signing up was no kind of decision. I just did it. Wouldn't nobody dare to question my reasons for fear of sounding unpatriotic. I told everbody I was going to do my duty, and help my brother while I was about it. I even quoted the Bible at least once that I remember, talking about "an eye for an eye" and about wanting to smite some Japs. Truth was, a course, I was running away just as fast and hard as I could.

When I signed up, I expected they'd give me a uniform and teach me to fly in a couple of weeks, and I'd be off killing Japs before Valentine's Day. Turned out so many fellows signed up to be pilots, they sent most of us home and said they'd call us when they needed us. That was okay by me—I could make my contribution to the war effort delivering iceboxes in Smackover—but ever time I begun to feel pretty good about not having to report to spring training, I sunk on back down thinking about Jugs out there in amongst all that fighting. The day they bombed Pearl Harbor was plumb awful. It was a mighty relief to find out the *Enterprise* had got loose and that Jugs was all right.

Who I felt the worst for was Dixie. A housewife without house nor husband. It wasn't long before that baby was coming, and on top of everything else, she had to worry about Jugs getting killed. I don't believe she'd have worried near as much if Jugs had wrote her what he was thinking in his letters. But, I reckon to keep her mind at ease, he wrote funny stuff. Made it seem like he wasn't being careful, but I knew he was, and I tried to make Dixie's mind easier.

In March of '42, Dixie had a little baby boy. Just like they promised, she named it after me. I told her not to feel like she had to do that, but she said her and Jugs wouldn't have it no other way. Andrew Jackson Fielder II come more than a month early, and scared everbody half to death. The doctors in El Dorado kept him in the hospital for three weeks and a little. When they finally let him loose, he seemed like he was okay.

I got word about little Jackson going home the day I reported to Nashville for six weeks worth of testing to see would I be a navigator, bombardier, or pilot. My high school teachers would have started building a bomb shelter if they knew I was smart enough to qualify for all three, but that I did, and I left for basic flight training at Maxwell Field in Montgomery, waiting around for the Army to decide what position they wanted me to play.

They passed on President Roosevelt's decision to me at the end of three month's basic: I was going to make a pilot like Jugs. It seemed right that if he was one, I'd be one, because we always done everthing together. I went through primary flight training at Carlstrom Field in Arcadia, Florida, then to Bainbridge, Georgia, for my advanced. Join the Army, see the U.S. of A.

I was a pretty fair pilot, but the Army Air Corps done one thing wrong. They told me that nigh on nine out of ten that tried to make pilot was washed out for one reason or another. I could not get this out of my head. I knew I was going to choke. Whenever I messed up, I told myself how I didn't really like flying all that much, which was a straight-out lie. Truth to tell, flying was as fun as pitching. My real problem was I wasn't doing bad enough to get canned quick, and I couldn't handle the pressure.

I took to reading the horrorscopes in the paper, looking for I don't know what. Finally, I got one that said, "Adventurous travel may lead to tragedy. Stay close to home." I showed it off around the barracks. It spooked me. When I messed up a training run that afternoon, I told my instructor what was bothering me. He didn't say a thing and I felt a fool. I decided to go ahead on and stick it out and let the chips fall. I kept the horrorscope in my pocket.

Little Jackson was in and out of the El Dorado Hospital for months, with first one thing and then the other. The doctors said if he could make it through the first year, he'd live to be a hundred.

It was February of forty-three, not too long after little Jackson went home from the hospital, my C.O. come and got me one night saying he had some bad news. I couldn't believe little Jackson had died, and him just a few weeks short of a year and everbody saying he was all right, and Dixie being on such hard times as it was. It didn't seem fair.

But it wasn't little Jackson. It was Jugs. The *Enterprise* was supporting the Marines' operations on Guadalcanal, and Jugs bought it on a milk run. He was lost at sea and presumed dead. My C.O. said them Navy pilots done a heck of a job against the Japanese and saved a many Marine. He said I ought to be proud of my brother.

I always had been.

That was the awfullest night of my life.

They let me go home for Jugs's service. You never seen a more pitiful sight than Dixie standing there with that teensey-tinesey baby in her arms, trying not to cry but tears rolling down her face and dripping on that baby. I couldn't look at her, else I knew I'd start bawling. Poor Maw was hurting pretty bad, too, and Jude. Shoot, it hurt the whole town. Jugs was the first fellow killed in the war from the county, and plus everbody knew him and loved him like a son. We buried a empty box next to Pa. I wanted to jump in the hole with it.

You know, bad stuff happening seemed to kindly build Jude up, like when Paw passed and he rushed out the church to call Lilly names and defend our Maw's honor. This time, the night after the service for Jugs, he come up to me and said that what with me gone, he was now the man of the house. I told him congratulations. He told me he was gonna start running the furniture store with Uncle Woodley. I wished him all the luck in the world. He told me he was gonna take care of Dixie and

Little Jackson. I told him to mind his own business, or me and him was going to war.

It was well after the funeral service before I talked to Dixie. She come to me and wanted to talk about Jugs. She knew that out of all the people in the world, I'd be the last one to forget Jugs besides herself. She asked me would I promise to tell little Jackson all about Jugs when he got old enough to listen. I promised. I told Dixie I'd see to it her and little Jackson would never have to want for nothing, but with her daddy being a oil-patch chiropractor, I knew she wasn't really worried about that.

I near about asked her would she want me to marry her. We was close enough that I thought I could, but I didn't. I went back to Georgia with a hole in me bigger than from losing the pennant.

When I got back to training school, I didn't have no more interest in flying a plane. I didn't even want to fight. The Japs had killed my brother, and they had won the war as far as I was concerned. I couldn't do nothing that would even start to get back at them for what they had done to my brother and Dixie and little Jackson—and me.

I missed a week of testing going back for the funeral, and they said I had to go through the three-month advanced again. I asked my C.O. what would happen if I didn't, and he got mad and told me they'd find something for me to do with my time. They did. They had me waiting hand and foot on the flight instructors there at Bainbridge. I polished shoes, washed cars, even carried their golf clubs on the weekends. It wasn't until February '44, one year to the day after I washed out of pilot training, my C.O. come asked me did I want to be a airman or a butler. By that time, I'd rather have been a kamikaze pilot than what I was. They transferred me to gunnery school at Fort Myers, Florida.

I liked shooting guns. Wasn't no guns in the house when we was growing up, which might have been why I liked them so much. Plus, I was pretty good at it. I had two good eyes back then.

10

Jugs would of laughed until the snot run if he knew I was in gunnery school. He was with me the one and only time I'd ever shot a gun. When I was ten, Paw got invited to go to a deer hunt in Louisiana. He took Jugs and me, saying it was time we learned about guns, several of which he borried from my uncle.

We was mighty excited about that hunting trip. Wasn't often Paw taken us anywhere, just us, without Maw and Jude. It was the first time for us to leave Arkansas.

The camp was on a white shell road, the like of which I had never seen, and it was way back in the woods, even for Louisiana. Must a been a dozen men there, but we was the only kids. It was November and real cold, and there wasn't no facilities. The men spit in the corner of the room. Everything was dirty, even what they ate. Me and Jugs was bug-eyed. We got the feeling the men figured us for sissies that didn't know much about guns, hunting, spitting, cussing, grunting, scratching, or trick urinating.

The men went to their deer stands before dawn and woke us up mid-morning when they begun coming in. We watched them dress the two deers they killed. Then about noon, Paw and them asked us if we wanted to go rabbit hunting. A course we did and we listened carefully while they showed us how to load and fire and work the safety on these two little four-ten shotguns.

We set out from camp stalking the fierce cottontail bunny. We stomped around in the woods for I bet three hours before Jugs finally shot a oak leaf just to break the ice. Not long afterwards, Jugs scared up a jackrabbit that tore past me in a panic. I squeezed off a shot from the hip, and as the gun butt was rupturing my spleen, I seen the poor bunny flip over, deader than dirt.

Neither Jugs nor me could believe our luck. We was some kind of hunter-men. We gutted the rabbit right there and took turns carrying it. We couldn't wait to show the menfolk back at camp. Course, we was delayed a little bit getting back to camp because we didn't have no idea where we nor the camp neither one was. After a while, we found the shell road and followed it back to camp.

The men was happy to see us and made us feel like a regular pair of Frank Bucks fresh off a safari. They passed the rabbit around, pointing out all its fine qualities. Said we ought to have it stuffed and mounted. When we told them how we got it, they said it was probably charging, and it was a good thing I killed it before it got to me. Jugs and me and Paw was about to bust with pride.

Then one of the older men started feeling up the rabbit's neck and got a terrible worried look. Everbody hushed. They passed the rabbit around again, each one of 'em feeling up under its neck and shaking their heads like you might do if you found out your aunt's dying.

Finally, Jugs couldn't stand it no more and asked the man that started the head shaking what the matter was. In a slow, low voice, he said he had felt and the rabbit's nymphus glands was swollen. This meant it probably had Alabama Spotted Blue-Tick Fever. *"The blue plague,"* one of the other old codgers whispered. He said we didn't have nothing to worry about unless we got any of the rabbit's blood on us. Jugs and me both looked at our hands. They was covered with blood up to the elbows. One of Jugs' ears was all red from where I hit him with a rabbit organ from about thirty feet.

We was doomed. I felt sick to my stomach. I remember looking right into that old man's eyes and asking, "Will the fever kill you?" He looked right back into mine and said, "No son, it won't kill you—but it'll make you wish you was dead." I sat down and started whimpering like a gutshot Yankee.

Jugs asked him, "Ain't there nothing we can do?"

The man said there wasn't but one hope. He couldn't tell for *sure* if the rabbit had the fever less'n he examined its liver. If its liver was spotted, it was okay. If it was striped, it meant "the fever—the *blue plague!*"

Jugs and me run off into the woods. We looked till it got too dark to see our feet for where we had shot that rabbit. No luck. We was goners. Our crotches begun to itch, which we sure-Lord believed must of been the first symptom of the fever. It was just red bugs, but we didn't know that yet.

It was dark when we found our way back to the deer camp. When we dragged ass in, the men busted out laughing. One or two was actually rolling on the floor, never mind the cigarette butts and general mess. Our own father, still laughing and tears rolling down his cheeks, come up and told us the men had played a little joke on us. I looked around for a loaded shotgun. Them men do not know how lucky they was I didn't find one. That night, evertime one of the men looked at us, he'd go to snickering, which would start everbody up all over.

Why it is that red bugs zero in on one part of your body, especially that part, is one of nature's little mysteries, I reckon. Or maybe it's one of *God's* jokes. Neither Jugs nor me could sleep for the itching. We was a pair a miserable younguns.

Jugs come got me up in the middle of the night. He put on a pair of gloves and give me one. He took a big hunting knife off the counter. I figured he wanted to slit some of the men's thoats in their sleep and didn't want to leave no fingerprints. I was all for it. We tippy-toed outside.

We went out to this big oak tree in front of the camp. He pulled off some vines which we taken around to the back porch. We picked all the leaves off the vine and Jugs chopped them up to pert near a powder. We tippy-toed back inside and sprinkled the powder on all of them men, even Paw.

Next morning, they looked like somebody pumped about twenty pounds too much air pressure into their heads. They eyes was swole shut and runny. And they was itching just a *whole* lot worser than we was. They figured they must of all got into some poison oak. They was right. Jugs and me didn't laugh then, but I can tell you we laughed many a time after.

❖ ❖ ❖

It wasn't too long after they finished mopping up Guadalcanal that they confirmed Jugs had been killed. Somebody in his squadron had seen his plane explode before it hit the water. They told us his last radio transmission was, "Don't worry about me, fellows, I can walk back from here."

You know, I ain't told that bunny story for a while. I used to just hear the jokes in it—theirs on us and ours on them and God's on all of us.

11

I don't know how much you know about the Air Corps part of the Army, Major, but you can't believe what we went through before we ever got to hit a lick at the first Jap. To fly on a 29, everbody had to have a dual rating and gunnery training except the pilots. All they had to learn was how to fly the plane. After gunnery school, I went through another three months of navigation training at Monroe, Louisiana. Even though Monroe was close to Smackover, I didn't go back after Jugs died. I don't know why, I just didn't.

Went to Great Bend, Kansas, to do my cross-country, which we had to do in 17s because they didn't have enough 29s. It wasn't until we got to Kearney, Nebraska, for our three-months overseas training that I first got to sit in a Superfortress.

The only time I been called in front of outside officers before today is when my crew accidentally, on a nighttime training mission, bombed Andros Island in the Bahamas instead of Isle of Pines off Cuba. We did fine from Nebraska until we crossed the Florida panhandle and took a wrong turn. But nobody got hurt, the Army paid for some crops, and the crew was all the closer for having flew through the storm.

The crew of a Superfortress is sort of like a baseball team: every man has got his job to do, and if everbody does it, ya'll are all all right unless it just ain't to be. Our crew was a whole lot closer even than any baseball team I'd ever played on. I reckon that's due to the fact that if you mess up in a baseball game, the worse you can lose is a pennant.

And just like in baseball, folks has got nicknames. It wasn't until we got in trouble for bombing the Bahamas that somebody found out I was "Gooseball." Before that they called me "Smackover." Anybody old enough to talk plain knew the story of Gooseball Fielder and the '41 pennant boner. Folks thought it was funny, excepting my own crew. They took up for me in public. I couldn't tell if it was team spirit or if they was kindly nervous about having a choker on their crew. They never did say nothing about it, but I suspected they didn't have the same confidence in Gooseball as they had in Smackover. And they might of been right to think that way, I don't know.

We trained and we tested and we trained some more. I wound up as a top turret gunner on a B-29 Superfortress. It taken over three years from when I joined the Army Air Corps until I flew my first mission against the Japanese. Seems like with a war going on they could have got us over there sooner, but that's the way the Army is. Suited me fine. I had spent three years with no pressure on me at all, at least not after I washed out of flight school. The Army took care of it all—they told me when to wake up, when to eat, what to do, when to hit the sack. Just what I wanted.

In February of '45, we left the States in a B-29 heading to the Mariannas. Our plane was named the "Miss Hap" after our boss, General Arnold. Some officer got the idea this might be offensive to the General, seeing how they was also a naked woman painted above the name. We changed the name to the "Miss Take," but we left the naked woman. We was going to raise hell and put a chunk under it.

Our first mission was bombing Okinawa before the landing. I was the central fire control gunner and sat on the barber chair right below the top sighting blister. I thought I was powerful scared in a major league bullpin, but it wasn't nothing up against riding in a top turret of a B-29 with Zeros, Zekes, and Tojos coming head-on at you firing tracers. The tracers would look like they was heading straight at your head until the last minute, when they would veer off—if you was lucky.

At first, I'd be ducking my head all around, dodging them bullets. I even kept my teeth clamped shut for fear of catching one down the gullet. After a while, I quit. After a while, you'd just try your hardest not to let it worry you. But you couldn't. So you just stayed scared. And you hated going up. And you hoped something not too bad would happen to your plane that would make you land on one of them little islands and you'd have to live out the war eating coconuts and hula dancing with women in grass skirts. But you knew deep down that what was really going to happen was you'd get shot down and killed in a fireball explosion like you seen every mission. And you couldn't stop thinking about it, stop wondering how it would feel to burn. Now, the Japanese got this soldiering mess figured out. Before a Japanese soldier goes off to war, they have him a funeral right then and there. He's dead from the time he leaves home. If he makes it back alive, that's gravy.

On March 5, 1945, we flew our first mission over downtown Tokyo from our base on Tinian. Before then, I'd worried about doing my job on my guns and hadn't thought too much about where the bombs fell. This time, though, when we was making our turn to head home after the bombing run, I looked down and seen a baseball diamond, bigger than Dallas. I couldn't hardly believe it. What was a baseball diamond doing in Japan? Back on Tinian, I asked, and come to find out, the Japs was big baseball fans with their own professional teams that wore uniforms just like ours. Why, Babe Ruth and a bunch of other major league players had been to Japan before the War to play the Japanese All-Stars.

All at once, I got to thinking that maybe the Japs was human beings. Ever since they bombed Pearl Harbor, we'd been told they was yellow, buck-toothed, conniving devils what ate their own young and anybody else's they could get a hold to. But if they played baseball, didn't they *have* to be just a little bit human?

Once, on a long train ride back from somewhere, I asked Neckless how he ever come to take a monkey for a pet. He said he'd been crazy about monkeys since he was a little fellow, and him and his paw used to go every fall to the Louisiana State Fair in Baton Rouge and hang out at the Orangutan Wrestling tent.

To hear him tell it, there was this orangutan about four-and-a-half foot high and four-and-a-half-foot wide, weighing in at five hundred pounds or so, with arms six foot long each. Grown men paid ten bucks to go in the cage on the chance they'd win a hundred if they could last three minutes. You didn't have to pin him or nothing; you didn't even have to stay *alive;* all you had to do was just to keep from getting thowed out. The cage was about fifteen foot around and six foot high with a big creosote pole in the middle holding up the tent. The pole was wore a little thin toward the bottom.

There wasn't but two ways to win the prize money, which no one ever done in all the years Neckless went to the fair. You could run around like a chicken with its head cut off—but the ape was quicker and it wouldn't be long before you was flying over the bars hoping to land on the fattest man in the bleachers. The other way was to latch on to the pole with all four sets of nails—but it wouldn't be long before the monkey pried you loose and sent you sailing. If you hung on *too* tight, you run the risk of the monkey tearing off a loose body part, which tended to break a man's concentration.

When you paid your money to wrestle, the monkey man give you a yellow coat to wear supposedly so as you wouldn't ruin your clothes, but really it was how he made the monkey patriotic. Neckless said as time went by they give you a football helmet, too, because the monkey got lazy and figured out if he just tore off a ear, chances were the human being would climb out the ring on his own.

Neckless said he quit going altogether after he snuck into the tent early one afternoon and seen the monkey man training the poor old orangutan. Seems he would put on the yellow coat and the helmet and whup the chained-up ape with a baseball bat.

I know the Japs picked the fight with us and no doubt there was some bad ones amongst 'em. Still, I got to thinking that all that yellow-devil talk about how evil they all was might be somebody's way of putting the yellow coat on them.

After that, I took to looking for baseball fields every time we flew a mission. Got to be a little game amongst the crew about who could spot the diamonds first.

On April Fools Day, nineteen and forty-five, which was a year ago yesterday as a matter of fact, we had just dropped a load of incendiaries on Tokyo and was making the turn when a line of Zeros appeared on the horizon at twelve o'clock low. Everbody was yacking on the radio and I was whizzing around in the barber chair, goosenecking every which way in my topside bubble, trying to see something to shoot at. There was about a dozen of 'em heading straight at us, so they said. I knew they was coming, and I was looking, but I just couldn't see 'em. Then I heard that God-awful hail-on-a-tin roof sound, and bullets was going through us. Hearing them bullets hit the plane and not being able to see the Zeroes was a whole lots worse than watching tracers heading for your nose.

I seen one Zero pass just overhead, and I heard a crash and seen a bright flash down below me in the fuselage. I started down off the barber chair to see if there was a fire, and there was another flash. Bullets smashed my plexiglass bubble and the pressure popped me out of the plane like a champagne cork. Everything got hotter than the hinges of hell, and then just as cold. I was spinning a hundred times faster than I could in that chair. I had to keep my eyelids shut tight, else my eyeballs would have slung out of my head. It come to me that I was spinning without no plane. One minute, I was in it; the next minute, I was floating in the middle of a bright blue sky watching the

Miss Take and the formation get smaller and smaller with Japan coming fast up to meet me. If my spinning hadn't slowed down, I'd have probably blacked out. As it was, I was able to grab the ring and yank open my chute.

It's funny what you think about when something happens to you like that, something that blows you out of your world. I didn't think about whether I was going to get killed in a tree or shot coming down or taken as a prisoner of war. All I could think about was getting in trouble for undoing my safety harness. I looked around. It felt real bad that I was the only chute in the sky. Maybe had I seen the Zero that popped my bubble, I could have chalked it. Hard to say.

I sure didn't feel like fighting when I hit the ground. All of a sudden I was real tired of war. I landed in a field smack dab in the middle of Japan. The field looked like it had been plowed, but there wasn't nothing coming up yet. I guess looking back maybe I should have gathered my chute up and hid out in the nearest swamp until the war was over. If I had of, it would of turned out a whole lot better for me, lifewise. But I didn't make no big effort to get away.

I checked myself all over to make sure I was all right. I was. A little singed but not overdone. I rolled up my chute, got my bearings, and started walking to the nearest road. I hadn't even made it out of the field when a half-track full of Japs drove up.

I reckon I ought to have put my hands up right when they started at me, but it kindly aggravated me that they was making such a fuss. Yonder I was, one airman in the middle of Japan without so much as a pocket knife, and they was carrying on like I was the first wave of the invasion. I guess me not offering to lick their boots right away chapped them a little, so they made me lie face down and get dirty before they shook me around and tied my hands together and threw me into a truck. A rattletrap little truck it was, too.

I felt like telling them if they'd just let me go home, I'd promise not to drop no more bombs on 'em. It wasn't that I was scared. I wasn't. I was scared when those bullets started raining through the plane; I was scared when my bubble blew out, and I was scared when I thought my eyes was going to be ripped from their sockets. But I wasn't scared of the Japanese. Maybe I should've been, but I wasn't. I was just tired.

We knew the Japs was bad on prisoners of war. We had heard stories from the Philippines and them other places about the torture and the bad conditions. But that was all from when the Japs was kicking tail. I'd flown five missions over Japan myself and knew of hundreds more. There wasn't much left of the cities. They had to know they was beat by now. I figured they would have to be downright crazy to mistreat prisoners.

After being hollered at in Japanese by six or seven officers somewhere, I was finally taken to a compound out in the middle of nowhere. They was bob wire and guard towers, pretty much what I expected. They took me to the Commandant of the camp. He wore glasses and didn't look to be in real good health. Had a bad cough and his eyes was kindly sunk back in his head. He also had the flattest haircut I ever seen. He could talk some English, enough to let me know what a cowardly dog I was and how I'd be digging latrines for the brave Japanese soldiers when they invaded California. As if. I did turn out to be smart enough not to question what he was saying, regardless of him being half my size. I just wanted to stay alive until the Marines come and rescued me and busted his chops.

The Commandant let me know how it would be so much better for me if I cooperated. So help me, I never did find out what he meant by that. I didn't really know too much, anyway. All I could have told him, even if I wanted to, was that we was going to bomb them today, tomorrow, the next day, and every day after that till they thowed in the towel. Besides that, I didn't know nothing but my name, rank, and serial number.

The barracks was more or less quonset huts. Probably less than more. Conditions was pitiful. The one the Japanese put me in must of had pallets for about thirty boys to sleep on the ground. The place stunk. The GIs was skinny and shriveled up, eyes big in bony faces. There was flies buzzing everywhere. Enough to break your heart or make you thow up, one. I couldn't hardly stand it. I was looking around, shaking inside, and all at once I saw it different and laughed out loud. All them hollow eyes swung around slow toward me, and I shook my head, embarrassed.

See, it reminded me of the junior high science fair, which was the first time I really knew for sure that my brother Jude's peculiarishness was more or less permanent. He had read where you could freeze a fish and thaw it out and it would come back to life. I reckon everbody has heard that, but leave it to Jude to think it on through. He got the idea it was more than likely that way with other kind of lower life, so he set out to do a scientific experiment to prove others of God's creatures could survive being froze.

Spent a month rounding up little critters. Soon as he got 'em, he'd put them in mason jars and take them over to the icehouse. After about a month of crawling under houses and up trees, he had a dozen mason jars full of all kind of creatures, especially lizards.

A week before the science fair, he went to building a tiny little outdoor park. He made it out of clay, string, branches, rocks, and scrap lumber. It had pine trees, hills, even a pond made out of the dog's dinner bowl. I will admit that the little park looked like a place I'd want to be in was I a lizard. Like a little bitty Central Park.

By the way, I don't think the dog would have minded giving up his bowl if he'd known he was almost the first critter in the deep freeze. He would have been, too, if Jugs hadn't asked Jude what he was toting off to the icehouse in that big cardboard box.

Well, the morning of the fair, Paw drove us to school in the store truck so we could tote Jude's lizard park. We set the "Lazy Lizard Dude Ranch" up in the gym along with the other kids' experiments. It was right off the most popular exhibit even without no animals in it yet. The kids come around just to admire the scenery.

I had lucked out on my own experiment for the fair. While Jude was building his lizard park, I was playing around and accidentally made something with some leftover clay that looked sort of like a face, and the face looked sort of like the pictures of cavemen in my science book. So I scooped it up, put it on a pie plate and turned it in as a Cro-Magnon man. I got a C for two minutes' work.

Now Jude couldn't have just showed up at school with a lizard ranch full of live lizards. The teachers'd surely accuse him of just catching 'em and keeping 'em at room temperature. For the experiment to prove something, them lizards was going to have to thaw out while the teachers was watching.

The judging and grading of the experiments was to happen after lunch. I went with Jude to the icehouse during lunchtime to help him get his jars. Once I seen the lizards, I knew this was going to be almost as good as the first Easter if these things ever crawled again. They wasn't green nor brown; they had kindly a clearish, gray color. They was all sunk in and it looked like somebody had popped their eyes out. A whole lot like them boys in the POW camp. Jude wasn't worried.

Well, we rushed the jars back to school and showed 'em to Jude's teacher. She was eating lunch at the time, and I could tell by the little urping noise she made that her and me was thinking just about the same thing. Jude climbed up on top of the table where his lizard ranch set and started to place the lizards all around the ranch in outdoorsy poses. A couple was up in a pine-branch tree. Five or six looked like they was playing "Follow the Leader." And a couple was drinking out of the dog bowl pond. In the scene that was my idea, four of the lizards had surrounded a froze june bug. I kindly wanted to see what'd happen when they thawed out and seen lunch setting right in front of 'em.

Well, it wasn't too long before the lizards was sweating. Water begun to bead up on their little noses. Jude took this as his first sign of success.

When the teachers come down to grade Jude's exhibit, not a creature was stirring, not even a roach, so they promised to come back in a while. After about a half hour, Jude was sweating hisself. He climbed back up by the ranch and taken the "Follow the Leader" lizards for a dip in the pond. This didn't soften 'em up any. He snapped a front leg off of one trying to exercise it back to life. He asked me to go get him some glue.

There *was* some sign of life in the ranch now, though. It's just that Jude hadn't collected no blue-tailed flies. They was swarming all over the ranch like tee-tiny buzzards.

The teachers come back around once more and finally convinced Jude them lizards was going to need more than a little time to get over their chill. Mr. Kincaid suggested putting up a lightning rod like they done in the monster pictures. I suggested taking 'em to a tent revival. Mrs. Pegues was trying so hard not to laugh, she snorted like a sow. A course, Jude started sniveling. One of the girls in Jude's class who knew a little something about pity led us all in a silent prayer for the reptiles what had give their lives in the pursuit of science.

I waited with Jude till Pa picked us up after school and we took the "Lazy Lizard Dude Ranch" home. The flies kept up with the truck on the way home, which give me the idea for my next science fair project: the speed of flies. We turned the park over in the back yard, and it stood up with "trees" for legs. It made a real nice sun shade for the dog. With thawed-out frozen snacks.

I did feel pretty bad for Jude, all the way until I told Jugs what happened. He was at the high school now, and counted on me to keep him up with the goings on at the junior high. I don't believe we ever laughed harder than we did that night. It become known around our house as Jude's Dud Ranch.

I reckon if one of them lizards had drunk a little water out of the dog-bowl pond, Jude would've become a scientist. Instead, he turned his mind to crime and become a profiteer. Let me tell you, we was all the worse for that.

12

All the POWs seemed to be airmen of one kind or the other. Ever one wore his uniform, or bits and pieces of what was left of it. The ranking officer was Colonel Cole.

This Colonel Cole, you was either his lackey or you was nothing.

Later on, when I was in the prison infirmary, there was a young fellow, a flyer, in the bed next to me, and he was burnt awful bad. He was dying, probably not fast enough to suit him, the way he was suffering. I ain't never seen a man in more pain. I talked to him some before he died. He knew it was coming. All he was worried about was being forgot after he died. After saving their souls, this is what dying soldiers think about mostly.

Colonel Cole was making the rounds of the infirmary and come to this flyer's bed. The boy starts asking if the Colonel will be sure his mother gets his Purple Heart and if the Colonel will write his family and tell them he was a good soldier. In the middle of this pitiful begging, Colonel Cole gets a note handed to him, and without so much as a word, he walks off reading his letter. I saw that poor boy's heart break. He died a hour later.

Me, I didn't think too much of Colonel Cole after I got a chance to know him a little. I imagine he told the Army what he thinks of me.

I could tell he was a Yankee quick as he opened the side of his mouth. He no sooner got my name than he begun telling me how the cow ate the cabbage. Launched into this big, long speech about the fortunes of war and how it was important for us to consider ourselves a second front. He told me it was essential that we contribute to the war effort, and everyone had a job to do. It was the "sermon on the mound" all over again.

I reckon the sermon was supposed to fire me up so I'd run out and hop the fence, fight my way into Tokyo, climb the wall of the Royal Palace, and stab old Hirohito hisself in the eye with a sharp stick. It was wasted on me. I wasn't in the mood. Don't get me wrong, I didn't like the Japs—they killed my brother—and I wasn't crazy about being in that prison, neither. But I been knocked out of ballgames before. When the manager comes to the mound and tells you you ain't got your stuff that day, there ain't no sense in making him wrestle you down and take the ball away. It's best just to give it up and come back another day. I wasn't no coward; I just didn't see nothing to be gained.

He ended his pep talk by asking me if I was brave enough to join his second front. I said I was, and in the same breath I asked him where I was supposed to sleep. That really burned him up. I started to apologize when I seen how mad he got, but I figured we'd be seeing enough of each other that I'd work an apology into the conversation in the next year or so.

I didn't sleep real well the first night. Somebody kept banging on a bell or a gong or something. The next morning, one of our officers woke me up early and said I needed to muck out the latrines. It seems like the Japs was kindly short-handed, and the POWs did most of everything, including policing their own.

Colonel Cole caught me at breakfast and said he had a job for me. Being as how I'd just mucked out the latrines, I figured whatever it was had to be a promotion. He told me about one of his officers who'd been caught trying to escape and been in solitary for four days. Said it was important to his second front for us to rescue this fellow from solitary. I was all for that, though I didn't know where we was going to rescue him to. I felt a little bit bad about how I hadn't got more excited the night before at his pep rally—even though I wasn't *that* much more excited the next morning—and I told him I'd do whatever I could to help.

Colonel Cole said there wasn't but only one lock-up, and if I was to get in trouble, the Japs would swap this other fellow out for me. He said this could best be done by a simple act of disobedience. He said since I was the new kid, the Japanese wouldn't be so hard on me, and I'd be out the next day, probably.

I got to thinking maybe I had messed up saying I'd help, but I had kindly backed myself in a corner. Another one of them patented Gooseball Fielder decisions.

The good Colonel told me I should demand to see the Commandant and not stop demanding until the Japs got good and aggravated. After being patted on the back by all the officers, I set off down the little main street to the Commandant's headquarters. I passed a few guards on the way that looked at me funny but didn't stop me. I was the only POW out and around, and they must have figured I was going somewhere where I was supposed to.

I walked and walked waiting for somebody to ask me where I was going, but nobody did. I walked right up to the Commandant's quarters, and there wasn't no guards like there was the day before. I didn't know what to do. I looked around and decided I'd go on in. That was surely one of the worst mistakes I ever did make.

I didn't get in the place more than a step or two when it hit the fan. Guards was screeching and carrying on, and somebody hit me square between the shoulder blades with a rifle butt and knocked me down. Somebody else kicked me in the side. I give up on breathing altogether. They rolled me over and a couple of 'em jumped on me.

At first I thought I'd just roll over and show 'em I wasn't no threat, but they kept on hitting me. Well, I says, to heck with this, there's enough of 'em that these little guys is liable to kill me if I just lay here. So I popped up off the floor and commenced hay-making, trying to fight my way back out of that place. It was a donnybrook, and for a few minutes I give back as good as I got. But even if I could've fought my way out, I didn't have no place in particular to escape to.

To make a short story long, I found out what that sorry-sounding gong was that kept me up all night the night before. It was "The Pipe," and the Japs used it as their solitary. Was just exactly what it sounds like. It was a piece of twenty-four-inch iron pipe, twenty or so foot long, sealed at one end. It was up off the ground and supported on either end by a couple of crossed pilings.

About six Jap guards marched me over to it, kicking me in the behind as we went. I didn't have no idea what it was at first. I only knew that it seemed like most of the stink I had smelled since I got to camp was coming from around it. I wasn't feeling too good having just gotten whupped, and the stink of that place made me want to thow up.

The Japs was screeching at me again, and I reckon they was telling me to take my clothes off, because no sooner had they started making a racket than they got aggravated and started tearing 'em off me theirselves. They stripped me buck naked, and one of 'em grabbed me by the hair of the head and shoved me towards that pipe. They wanted me to get *in* that thing.

Every ounce of sense in my body was telling me not to, but when you're buck naked surrounded by a swarm of Japs with rifles who are surrounded by bob wire on an island surrounded by the Pacific Ocean, you kindly have to do what you're told. To this day, I ain't sure it wouldn't of been better to see how far up the fence I could of climbed before they shot me down.

The pipe was raised about four feet off the ground, and being in the altogether, I had to raise myself up into it right carefully, if you know what I mean. It was narrow, hardly enough room for my shoulders to fit. You really needed a slipperslide to get in. There was a hole about four inches around midway down the pipe at the bottom. I didn't have to get too close to figure out the hole was the commode facilities, and the last guy in wasn't no bombardier. Plus, it was murdersome hot.

As long as I was crawling forward, I was all right. But when I'd crawled about as far as I could, I tried to look behind me. I couldn't. I couldn't get where I could get a good look out the other end of the pipe. And I couldn't turn around.

Something snapped inside of my head. I had to get out of that pipe. I started backing out like a crazed inchworm. I backed over the hole. I wasn't thinking no more, I was insane. Closetphobia they call it. That's psychology.

The Japs seen me coming out, and they was ready for me. They had 'em some bamboo sticks by the end of the pipe just for this occasion. I just got my bare behind out the end of that pipe when they begun whacking. It hurt, but I wasn't going back into that pipe. I fell out and fell on the ground, and they kept whacking away with them sticks. POW piñata. Next thing I recall, I was back in the pipe, coming to. I remember thinking I knew what a rat feels like at a rat killing.

I believe it was night when I woke up, and they had sealed off both ends of the pipe. The only air I had was through the toilet hole, and that air wasn't too fresh. I couldn't lie down comfortable because of the curve of the pipe. What I remember most about that first night, though, is feeling things crawling on me. I couldn't see 'em, but I could feel things crawling on me.

The next day, they stuck food and water into the pipe. They did that the next day and the next day and the next day. I just laid there. That's all you could do. First I was scared. I would think about how to get out. Then I would try to tell myself somebody was going to get me out. Then I would tell myself that I wasn't going to get out and I was going to die.

It went on day after day after day.

But I wasn't dying, leastwise not fast enough. I was dying slow. I could tell. My teeth got loose. I couldn't see straight no more. I couldn't tell what was stinking worser, the inside of the pipe or the outside of the pipe. If I tried moving much, my skin would just scrape off.

Most of what I thought about was crazy, but some of it was the stuff they always say you think about before you die. I thought about my life. I thought about how my brother had died and I'd never told him I loved him. Not once. I thought about his little son and how pitiful it was he wouldn't have no daddy and how he wouldn't have me for a uncle neither. I thought about how bad it was for my Maw to lose two of her sons to a war where we was fighting people that played baseball just like us.

Nothing made sense. I had worked my whole life to get to pitch in the major leagues, and I finally got there, and I ruint my life in five seconds with a bonehead choke. Now I was laying in a pipe halfway round the globe, just rotting away. And I wasn't but twenty-two years old.

About mid-morning, they'd open the end of the pipe to poke in a cup of rice soup. But, see, they couldn't just open the end of the pipe. They had to bang on it first. The banging made my loose teeth rattle, and it didn't do my ears no good, neither. I had trouble sleeping because of my ears ringing. I begun to worry that something was bad wrong with my brains.

After I'd been in there six days, I almost wished they hadn't of opened the pipe. In the little space of time it was open, I seen that what I'd hoped was the tingling of natural healing in all my cuts and scratches was really flies rooting. They was all over me. Now that I seen 'em, I expect I imagined more than was really on me. I can't tell you how this disgusted me. Being bad hurt was one thing, but having crawly things all over me, that was different and that was just too much. I tried to slap at 'em, to fan 'em away, to pluck 'em, to scrape 'em. I even gave up what passed for fresh air and covered up the hole by laying on it so no new flies could get in. It wasn't no use.

By the second week in the pipe, I had called myself a fool and told myself "I told you so" no less than ten thousand times. For a while, I kept expecting the Japs to come let me out. Every noise I heard, I stopped slapping at the flies and listened for the pipe to open. Every time they didn't open the pipe, it made me that little bit more suspicious they never would. Still, I was telling myself I'd live to laugh about all of this, and I was doing a pretty fair job of believing it.

By the start of the third week, I knew I had bought the farm. In fact, I *wanted* to die. By now, it seemed to me that even if I *did* get out, I would more than likely die of my wounds and infection without good medical treatment. See, it was just about the start of that third week that my mind kept coming back and back to the kitten I'd found back in Smackover when I was kid. I could hear myself mewling and see my eyesockets full of maggots. I couldn't stand to think about it, and I couldn't think about nothing else. I wasn't sure there was anybody going to put me out of my misery. And I had plumb forgot to pack my shovel.

You'd think that once I'd give up, that might of ended my misery. No such luck. It's harder to die than you think, especially when you ain't got a foot to kick your own bucket with. I had thought about killing myself when I first got home to Smackover after the New York game. I learned you can't drown yourself with a shower nozzle. But things was considerable worse in the pipe, and I decided to give it a heck of a try.

I quit eating. I quit swatting flies. I quit picking bugs off me. I even quit using the latrine as best I could. I just laid down and tried to die. This is done by repeating to yourself that you're getting weaker with each breath. Then you give your soul up to the Lord. Then you wait. And wait. Then your behind starts to itch, but you tell yourself not to scratch it because this will slow death down. Then one of them twin-engine flies lands on your lip and starts making a nest in your nose, but you tell yourself to let it be, death is near. Pretty soon you scratch your behind and snort the fly out and you got to start dying all over again.

I'd been in that pipe over three weeks and hadn't been able to die yet. I'd long since quit eating my rice. All I did was drink water and breathe. Cramps was goosestepping through my guts. My bottom half had a mind of its own, which happened to be the mind of a baby. I remembered my Maw telling me the worst thing in the world would be for a person to die in the hospital without nobody from the family there. Maw didn't have that quite right.

One particular morning, I started itching all over. Then my teeth started to rattle. Then it felt like my whole skeleton was vibrating. This was it. Death was like a jeep ride. Then I heard a noise. It was low at first, but it kept getting stronger and stronger. The whole *pipe* started shivering and then shaking, and I knew what it was; it was Superfortresses. Hundreds of 'em. Coming over in wave after gorgeous wave. In the distance, I could hear the bombs. It went on and on and on. And that blessed vibrating jarred me back to life.

I decided right then that I wasn't going to die. I didn't care *how* long they kept me in that pipe. One of these days, the Marines was going to come open it and I was going to pop out, get myself fixed up, and make something of my life. I was going to take care of my little nephew. I was going to marry Dixie. I didn't know if I could pitch again in the majors, but if I couldn't, I would pitch in the minors, and if I couldn't do that, I'd coach, and if I couldn't do *that,* I'd teach gym, and if I couldn't do none of it, at least I'd teach little Jackson to thow the gooseball. Pipe dreams. That's psychology.

Felt like every bomb that shook the pipe made me stronger. Made me proud. I might of been in that formation if I hadn't of been shot down. Now I was mad, *real* mad. It ain't in my nature to get angry, but by George, they had killed my brother and pert near had killed me, and I wasn't going to take it no more. I was going to win. I was going to live.

But life in the short run meant eating, swatting, plucking, and using the latrine. And luck was still running against me. The Japs figured since I ain't eaten in a few days, I'd died—or was at least past eating—and they quit bringing me food and water. I had been in the pipe twenty-five days, give or take.

I survived the last two days in the pipe by pitching ball games in my head. I had done it as a kid to pass time. You imagine getting a sign, taking a windup, and thowing. Then you think the ball into the mitt. It's either a ball or a strike. You keep count. There's lots of cheating goes on.

Something happened to me while I was pitching them games in my head. It was like getting religion. Not Bible religion. I had got that a dozen times or more. This was something new. I decided that while I had been pitching, my life was right. Everything wasn't perfect, but I knew I was on the right track. After I lost the pennant and decided not to pitch no more, the world had gone plumb crazy. There was the war, Jugs getting killed, and now me stuck in a pipe a million miles from a hot dog.

The more I thought about it, the more it made sense. If I ever got out of that pipe, I wasn't going to stop till I pitched again. In the majors. I was going to work out. I was going to get back in shape. I was going to get my head back in the game. Wasn't going to *be* no choking. Laying there in that pipe, I could feel the crowd in St. Louis yelling, "Gooooose!"

I was sleeping when they finally opened up the pipe to haul my bones out. I didn't wake up until I was in mid-air. The Japs had grabbed my ankles and jerked me out of the pipe so fast the metal scraped all the skin off my hip bones in the front. I was hollow enough by that time, I'm surprised I didn't pop like a light bulb when I hit the ground. Once they seen I was alive, they let some of the other POWs take me to the infirmary. The other fellows looked at me like I had looked at that little cat. I took this as a bad sign.

I reckon I had a pretty stout fever. I went back and forth between freezing and burning for days there in the infirmary. They couldn't do much for me except change my bandages. I hadn't never had no muscles to speak of, but now I looked like a red worm with the mud slung out of it. A waste of skin, way too much for what it had to hold.

The good Colonel come by, saluted me, shook my bony, scabby hand, and told me what a brave airman I was. He said he'd see to it I wasn't never forgot by the great people of the United States. I thought to myself that I had made sure of that four years ago in Yankee Stadium.

The fellow I bailed out of the pipe never did thank me. I guess he figured he was owed it. I seen him, though. Fat as a tick. All I could figure is he must of been a fly-eater. I didn't care that he never spoke to me. I didn't want no part of him, nor the Colonel, nor the Army, nor the war. I just wanted to get well, get back in shape, go home, and pitch again. And marry Dixie.

13

It took a couple of weeks but everbody finally quit looking at me like a maggot-eaten kitten. I took this as a good
sign. I was still puny, but feeling fair-to-middling. The day
come when I figured laying in the infirmary wasn't doing
me no good. I marched out past the fellow they called Doc.
He tried to talk me back to bed, but I waved him off. I'd
had plenty. I was fixing to start my comeback right then.
The Colonel hollered at me where was I going. Said I was
going to play ball. Now, mark my words. Them was my
words exactly.

I went out into the compound and picked up rocks.
When I had a shirttail full, I drawed me out a plate in the
dirt, and then a mound, and then I toed me a rubber. I
started pitching rocks against a circle on the latrine wall.
The fellows probably figured me for crazy as a bullbat.
Might of been. Might be yet. I didn't care—I had made
myself a promise. The Jap guards seemed to get a kick out
of my show. They didn't bother me.

The Colonel tried to talk to me when I come back in
the barracks. I acted like I was crazy and couldn't hear
him, and then I quit talking to anybody. I ate and slept to

myself. The Colonel give me the evil eye every chance he got. Fine with me. He never done me no favors, that's for sure.

Early one morning, everything started shaking again. Hot dog, the Superfortresses was back! Everbody, Japs and GIs and all, run out to see what was happening. Them planes was a sight. Must have been a thousand of 'em, and no resistance we could see. The bombs started dropping about two miles away. Smoke boiled up. I was so tickled, I started whooping. That was kindly dumb, since one of the first sporting lessons I learned growing up in south Arkansas was it ain't never a good idea to cheer too loud for the visiting team. Must be the same in Japan, because a Jap guard took offense at my cheering and decided to see could he knock my head off my skinny neck using his rifle as a bat. I was looking up and never seen it coming.

There was a loud crunch and a strange smell, and then the sun went out. Everything was black. Pain shot through my cheek. I wanted to cry. I wasn't going home. I couldn't feel nothing but my cheek, and it was killing me. I rubbed my tongue around the inside of my mouth to check for broke teeth. There weren't none broke nor chipped, but something was wrong. I slowly bit down on my teeth. It hurt, but there was also this grinding feeling. Something in my face was broke. I tried to open my eyes. I could see a little out of my left eye. Not my right. I must've blacked out after that.

I ain't never told no one before, but when I blacked out, I had a dream that I died. You know them dreams that feel like they really are real? Well, this one, I still don't know what to make of it. All the pain went away and I was plumb peaceful. Nothing mattered no more, not the

Japs, not the war, not baseball, not nothing. It wasn't like I didn't care, it was just that I knew it wasn't important.

Then—and if I'm lying, I'm dying—I *seen* myself laying out on the ground. The Jap guards was all around me, watching the bombers as they come over. I could see my eyeball was popped out of my head and hanging by a string. My cheek was bleeding. But I didn't hurt no more.

I rose up in the air and my body stayed on the ground. I got higher and higher. It was like I was heading home after a bombing run, but I wasn't in a plane. I had left my old wore-out body in the prison camp and seemed to have me a strong new one. I flew over cities with baseball diamonds and then out across the ocean, heading due east into the rising ball of the sun, faster and faster.

I seen a island coming up that I thought would be Midway, but it looked smaller. I slowed down and dropped lower as I come closer. On this island was one big tree, bigger than any you ever seen. Maybe big as a redwood, but branched like a oak. Under this tree was men and women, running around crazy, crying, jostling and bumping into one another. The women was pulling out their hair and ripping at their clothes. I never seen people so sad and wild.

When I got on the ground, I headed over to see what the matter was. The people was walking away from the tree shaking their heads, many of them crying, some with faces just gone stiff. I asked them what was wrong, but it was like they couldn't hear me for their grieving.

As I come up under the tree, I seen the most terrible sight. There was dead babies lying all under the tree. There was live babies in amongst the branches. The branches was loaded with babies and apples. The babies would reach for the apples, and when the stem would turn loose, the babies would come falling out of the tree and hit the ground with a sound like a watermelon when it drops off a truck. It made me sick.

I couldn't let them babies die. I seen one start to fall, and I went after him, hoping to catch him before he hit. But as he fell, I caught sight of another baby closer to me, and I forgot the first one and went after him. Then I heard one crying louder, and went for him, forgetting the one before. It was raining babies, and I couldn't catch a *one* because I couldn't make up my mind which one to catch. So I caught none. They just fell all around me. After a few minutes of doing no good at all, I started crying myself, but I couldn't give up. I kept trying, and I'd always get distracted. One baby hit right at my feet. I bent down over his crumpled little body, and I was crying hard as an April rain. My face started hurting.

The next thing I remember was in a Jap hospital ward with Jap nuns scurrying around. I hadn't never seen no Jap nuns before. They was short and at first they looked like cheap copies of real nuns—but they wasn't. They was real, as kind and caring as anybody could be, whatever their color or size.

I don't know how nor why I got took to the Jap hospital. I always wondered at them not just letting me die. Could've been them B-29's humming all around was kind of a conscience to the Japs. Could've been there was good ones and bad ones, just like in America. I don't know.

What the Jap guard had done was shatter my cheekbone. Turns out it don't break like you'd expect a bone to break, it breaks like a eggshell. Your cheekbone also holds your eye up, which I didn't know, and once the swelling went down, my right eye was drooping bad. I could see out of it, but since my eyes wasn't lined up, everything was double. The nuns bandaged it over, and so long as I didn't try to chew, I was okay.

Lying in that hospital bed, I didn't feel like I was fighting the war no more. It was like getting pulled from a game: You go into the locker room, take your shower and get dressed. All the while the game goes on, and you hear the crowd noise, but you feel different about it when you ain't playing.

There was burnt children and women in the beds all around me. I knew it was our incendiaries did it, and I reckon they couldn't hardly miss that I was the enemy. The 29s was flying over near about every day now. Seemed like the war was done for me, one way or the other. And I felt better.

I couldn't help thinking a lot about Dixie and little Jackson. Spent my days trying to imagine exactly what it was Dixie was doing back in Smackover. It was summer. She was more than likely listening to St. Louis play, sitting with her folks around the radio, with little Jackson—he'd be about three or so by now—playing with a toy plane or a baseball or something.

She'd have to pass by my house on her way to anywhere, so surely she thought about me every day. We was best friends long before Jugs ever give her a second thought. If I hadn't of been so set on playing baseball, she might of married me first. Like my granny used to say, you never know what's in the store for you. But now Dixie needed someone to take care of her and Jackson. I'd be more than glad to do that. It was the decent thing to do. I could make a good enough living at the furniture store.

One of the Japanese sisters come by one day with paper and pencil and a Red Cross envelope. I could of wrote Maw, but I might not have but one shot. I decided to take the long shot. Now, I'd wrote a good number of letters in my life, and I'd even wrote my share of theme papers and book reports in school, but let me tell you, you ain't wrote nothing till you try to convince a girl to marry you that you ain't seen in three years, that was married to your brother now deceased, and that is raising a boy named after you, all on one piece of paper with a pencil without no eraser.

I was first going to try and reason with her, tell her how much better off she'd be if she was married to me, but everything I thought to write come off like I had the swell head. Thought maybe I ought to tell her I loved her, but I couldn't come up with no reason why I had known her twenty years and just all-of-a-sudden felt in love with her that day. So I decided to tell her I had *always* loved her, and was just now telling her because it was the first time I'd had time to think things through. Once I got started, it even made sense to me. Maybe I had loved her all those years. It was possible. I reckon, looking back, I *was* a little ticked at Jugs when he married her. Whether I loved her or not, it was a fine letter even if I do say so myself. I didn't tell her nothing about my face.

A nurse come and took the letter in the afternoon. That night, I couldn't think of nothing else. I imagined the letter getting passed amongst Red Cross folks, each one more dedicated than the last as far as seeing that my letter got delivered. I fell asleep thinking about my new family and what good care I was going to take of 'em.

When I woke up the next morning, I was having some serious second thoughts. Had I wrote the right things? Maybe she never liked me at all but had just hung around me to be around Jugs. Maybe she thought I wasn't nothing but a green kid. Maybe I was. Maybe my head was shaped like a potato, and now it didn't have but one eye.

I was feeling pretty queasy by the time the Jap doctor come around. They unwrapped my eye. When I seen the expression on their faces once they peeled the bandage down, my stomach turned a back flip. The doctor told the nun to do something. She hesitated so he told her again, loud. She scurried off and come back with a mirror. I had to shut my right eye to see. I looked in the mirror. My face was all the colors in a oilslick. It was a mess.

The right eye was drooping and sort of bulging out of the socket. When I thought I was closing that bad eye, I wasn't really. The top lid was too short to reach the bottom lid. There was also stitches under my eye—not medical-type stitches but stitches like you'd see on a cheap basketball. It looked like they'd used a shoe string to sew me up. Otherwise, I resembled a rooster with the wart-head. I wasn't no looker to start with, but I never had people point at me neither. They was going to now.

And here I had just asked a good-looking girl to marry me. The same Red Cross workers I'd thought about handling my letter so careful I now hoped was goofballs, trailing dropped mail from here to home. Boy, I wanted that letter back. Didn't know what I was thinking when I sent it. If I ever got home, maybe I could claim the rifle butt in the head had knocked me nuts.

The doc, a old, bent-over Japanese fellow, left a big eyepatch-looking thing next to my bed. I studied it for a long time. Looked like half a brassiere. A popped-out eyeball held in by a brassiere. I wondered maybe if this wasn't God's way of punishing me for all the time I spent as a kid gawking at the women in the Sears catalog. I didn't want to wear it, but I didn't want my eye showing, neither. Finally, one of the nicer nuns come and tied it around my head. It worked okay. Covered my bad eye so I could see out the other. It was also big enough so you couldn't tell what a mess there was underneath.

The next morning, the hospital had a surprise inspection. The nuns who'd been flying around settled down, and the Jap patients started to sit or lay at attention. It was dead still when the doors to the ward was flung open. Two young Jap soldiers with rifles come in first and stood at attention just inside the swinging doors. Then come a Jap admiral walking like he knew where he was going. He was followed by a short, banjo-bellied Jap sailor that looked a lot like Curly on the Three Stooges.

The Jap admiral marched right up to the Mother Superior. She pointed at me, and here he come. Straight up to the foot of my bed. I wouldn't have thought I'd ever be scared again, but I could feel my heart about to bust out my chest.

My instincts was to jump up and salute him. Ain't that something? I swung my feet onto the floor and then I stopped. After all, it was the Japs had started this war, and it was the Japs had put me in the pipe for four weeks, and it was a Jap had teed off on my head with his rifle, so I wasn't going to jump up and salute a Jap even if he *was* a admiral, leastwise not till he made a fuss and insisted. Worst thing could happen would be he'd take that over-sized sword and chop my head off. At least then I wouldn't have to worry about that letter making it to Dixie.

He come right up and eyeballed me. In a minute, he give an order to one of the nuns, and she come over and took my patch off. By the look on his face, his raw-fish breakfast started swimming upstream on him when he seen my eye. He shook his head and walked out fast as he come in. Everbody was staring at me. I put my patch back on.

The rest of the day I spent studying about what that little visit might of meant. The nuns had pretty good poker faces most of the time, but now they was making a special effort not to look in my direction at all. I figured some-body had got the back end of their habit chewed on for taking care of a American flyer when we was raining hundredpounders all around. I figured I was either going back to the prison camp or I was going to be executed, one. The Japs was big on chopping off heads.

Well, at least I had got to pitch in the major leagues before I died. That's more than most poor dogfaces do before they check out. Things could be worse. I could of washed out in the minors and then died choking on a peppermint in the furniture store back in Smackover. I guess that would of been worse.

The next morning, I was picking at my face when the ward doors busted open again. This time, it was just Curly by hisself. He shoved a piece of paper at the Mother Superior and come after me. This was it. I didn't even bother sitting up. I might should of, because the first thing he done when he got to my bed was swat me on the top of the feet with a little buggy-whip switch he carried. It hurt like the dickens, and I popped up like a jack-in-the-box.

Even in his high-heeled boots, he was still a head and a half shorter than me, and I believe once this sunk in, it made him even testier. He went to hit me again, and I made another bad call. I caught his switch with my right hand just before it got to my left shoulder. He jerked it out of my hand the same time I let go, and his little switch skeetered across the tile floor and ended up under a bed on the other side of the ward. I could tell I was in bad trouble when I seen the nuns a-shoving one another trying to get out the door.

Curly's face was red as a Jap flag and he looked just short of foaming at the mouth. I could see he didn't know quite what to do, but I knew he couldn't let things stand as they was. I figured that before he thought of something worse, I might ought to give him a chance to save face. So I kindly shuffled over real easy to where his whip was, and bent down real slow to pick it up, giving him a nice target he couldn't let pass. WHOP! His boot caught me right in the split of my split-tail gown. I sprawled out on the floor just like the real Curly would of done if Moe had kicked him. I reckon he figured he'd got the best of me. Leastways, he didn't whup me no more, not for a while anyway.

I followed him out to a car with a little Jap flag where the hood ornament was sposed to be. He give me a used pair of brogans and made me walk down the dirt road in front of the car, away from the hospital and the nuns that had took such good care of me.

My legs was weak, and I surely looked a sight in brogans and that split-tail gown that was made for someone half my size. The only thing to really bother me was that every step I took jarred my eyeball socket. I kept on the eyeball brassiere the nuns give me, but it didn't really help with the pain. I tried walking softer, but that tired my legs out quicker, and I wasn't sure how far I was going to have to go.

Nor was I sure where I was going or why, except I guessed maybe I was fixing to cash it in. The Jap admiral probably blowed him a gasket when he found an American flyboy being nursed back to health in a Jap hospital, and he probably had in mind to do the honors personally.

I thought about running off in the beanfields next to the road, but I was tired. Not so much tired of walking or tired of hurting, which I was, but more tired of living in a world where folks do the kind of awful things they do to other folks. A fellow in New York that'd swear at a nineteen-year-old kid trying his best to pitch a baseball ain't too much different from a Jap that'd take a home-run cut with his rifle at a unarmed prisoner just out of a couple or four weeks in a pipe. I decided I didn't too much care if they killed me, long as they didn't mess with me. I wasn't in the mood.

After we'd gone about two miles, Curly blowed his horn and pointed for me to turn in a long driveway. At the end of the driveway was a great big house. It definitely wasn't no part of the prison camp.

14

Curly took and put me in a toolshed and brought me a Jap housecoat and a pair of knee-high britches. He thowed the clothes at me yelling something and kicked me when I bent down to pick 'em up. In the hospital, I knew it was coming and it didn't hurt too much, but here he caught me in a soft spot and it smarted like the dickens.

I stood and puffed myself up best I could. I was looking down at him and he decided right quick he didn't too much want to be in a little toolshed with me. He backed out the door and hollered some more. My eye socket was throbbing, and I saw him draw his sword. I hunkered down on a sack of something. He raised his sword over his head and come back in. I just watched. I was ready to watch him chop my head in half.

He might of done it, but the Admiral come out to check on the ruckus, I guess, and appeared over Curly's shoulder just in the nick. He put a stop to it with a word. Maybe two—hard for me to tell. Curly bowed at him and left the toolshed. The Admiral stepped in and stood over me. I noticed my whole self was trembling like a leaf.

Couldn't stop it. I looked at him, he looked at me. He didn't say a thing.

I reckon I was grateful he had kept Curly from halfing my head but I started to get aggravated at him staring. The fact I couldn't quit shaking like a wet dog made it worse. After a while, I looked at the ground instead of him. When I raised my head, he was gone.

I slept in the dirt in the toolshed amongst the rakes and hoes and shovels. There was a cane knife up on a shelf and some mason jars full of noxious smelling things. I remember thinking that if I still wanted to kick my own bucket, I had the stuff to do it with. I decided to sleep on it. Every time I woke up, I was shivering. I dreamed about the baby tree.

Curly woke me up in the morning with a kick in the head that set my face to burning again. I was hungry and my mouth was dryer than road dust. I hadn't had nothing to eat nor drink since I left the hospital. Curly wasn't no Florence Nightingale.

I got the feeling Curly was itching for me to try something. Had his rifle on his shoulder, a sidearm, and that little buggy-whip. Whenever I looked at him, he was staring a hole right through me. Seemed like for this fellow to hate me so bad, he must have *known* me. I couldn't place him though.

Before too long, the Admiral sent for me. Curly took me into the library, give me a juke in the ribs with his switch, and left. The Admiral looked me over again, up and down, like he was picking which cow to slaughter.

Then, in real good English, he said, "Sergeant, I do not wish to embarass you, but would you be so kind as to remove your bandage?"

I pulled the patch off. He seen what he asked to see, and then he shook his head and walked over and looked out the window. I held the patch back over my eye so I could see him.

"War is a terrible thing," he said with his back still to me. I'm thinking, *You're telling me, buddy. How come y'all had to start it?* He had a sad look on his face. Hurtful sad. For the first time in a long time, I thought about people having problems other than me. Seemed to me his problem might have been more than just his country playing all defense now.

He turned back away from the window all of a sudden and said, "Gooseball!" with a big grin.

I near about fell out.

"Gooseball?" he said again, slow, wondering if he'd got it right.

"Yeah," I says. "That's right. Who told you that?"

"Ah," he said and, God is my witness, he reached in his drawer and slapped a New York Yankee cap on his head. We both went to laughing. I laughed so hard my eye was running.

I couldn't believe it. He told me he was stationed in New York before the war and had seen me pitch in that last game of '41. Struck me kind of funny that after four years and several bombing runs over his country, I was still embarrassed at having blowed that game. Figure that. Shame-faced in front of a Jap admiral of the yellow Jap Navy that I was supposed to hate like the devil. Well, I reckon if the devil hisself told me he'd seen me pitch that game, I'd be embarrassed.

Yellow or not, the Admiral knew his baseball. We talked about some of his favorite players, mostly Yankees.

"You know, Admiral, I didn't know ya'll went in for baseball until I seen all the diamonds from the air." I didn't say I had been dropping incendiaries at the time, but I didn't have to. His smile disappeared all at once and he looked back out the window.

When he turned to me again, there wasn't no expression to speak of on his face. "Gooseball," he said, "you will stay here and care for the gardens."

So they wasn't going to kill me, not right off anyway. I was going to do some Japanese gardening. Old Curly was there to make sure it didn't get too relaxing.

You know, for a while I had been ready to die. *Hoping* to die, if you want to know the truth of it. I hadn't talked, or even much thought about baseball in the service because I was disgusted with myself for what I done. It took me being shut up in a pipe before I started thinking about baseball again. Even then, I only had myself to talk to about it, and it didn't last but until that rifle butt broke my face. Those few minutes I spent with the Admiral was joyful. Kindly reminded me of some stuff might be worth remembering.

The next day, laying on my back clipping some prickly little bushes while Curly snoozed under a tree, I happened to look at the house and something caught my eye. It was a youngun, a Japanese boy, staring at me out the window. Figured he must have been the Admiral's boy. Back home, a fellow that age would have been out playing on such a fine summer's day. I reckon with your pappy being a admiral and B29s coming over most every day now, it might look bad if you was having fun.

That kid set me to thinking how if the war hadn't come, I might have been playing ball back home myself. And Jugs might be listening to it with Dixie and little Jackson on the radio. The Admiral was right, and it ain't news: war is all the most terrible things rolled up in a great hurricane and turned loose on the world. But I don't have to tell you that, sir. I see you been there.

Seemed like I had just kind of been set on the bench. The war was over for me. It might still kill me, but I wasn't going down fighting. I'd be going down gardening.

I'd have been pert near happy except for Curly. It was like he had a bad tooth or something. Stayed sore as a boil. He'd yell and slap at my head and kick me ever chance he got. Even took to spitting on me fairly regular. Whatever was eating him, he must not have cared too much for his own safety, because he'd carry on like that, and me with a hoe or shovel in hand and having swung a bat or two in my day. He'd be a-yelling and I'd be picturing myself taking a home-run cut at his slick-bald head with my hoe and knocking it into the left centerfield stands.

I seen the kid nearly every day. He stayed inside mostly. He was a nice enough looking young fellow— taller than most of his people and filled out better, too. He was too young to be soldier but bigger than a lot of 'em I'd seen. He'd of made two of some of them guards at the prison camp, with enough left over for a fair-size child.

One afternoon when I was cleaning up a flower-bed deal—some of their flower beds didn't have nothing in 'em but rocks and maybe a tree—I heard something going *slap, slap, slap*. Wasn't but one noise sounded like that. I turned around to see. The boy was standing over a ways on a path and, sure enough, flicking a baseball into a glove.

I couldn't believe it. I'm raking pea gravel in a robe and knickers and this Jap kid's spudding around with a baseball and glove.

I rolled my shoulder a few times so as to let him know I was up to it. He starts thowing pop-ups to hisself, circling around under 'em. Finally he puts one in the gravel garden. Curly shoots him a cold stare and the kid acts like it's a accident, but he didn't fool me nor Curly, neither one. I was itching just to touch that ball. I raked myself on over to it. I leaned down to scoop it up, and before I could, Curly barked something at me. I froze. The boy spoke sharp to Curly, and Curly talked back. Then that boy got up in Curly's face like a manager does a umpire and let him have it with both barrels. I didn't have no idea what was being said but I knew whose side I was on. The boy got the last word. Curly walked off with his ears tucked back. The boy grabbed his ball and stormed off inside. I felt like laughing till Curly kicked me in the back of the leg.

The next morning Curly took me to the Admiral's library. The Admiral's son was there too. The boy shot Curly a dirty look and Curly showed hisself out of the room.

"Gooseball," the Admiral says. "This war will not last forever. Someday the bombs will stop falling and the baseballs will fly again."

I was counting on it. There was some gooseballs yet to be thowed.

He introduced his boy, Yoshi. "Yoshi is a fine pitcher, but there is much an American major league pitcher could teach him. It would be a great honor if you would help him become a very fine pitcher like yourself," he says.

It still kindly stretched my mind to picture Japs playing baseball, but anything to keep from weeding was
worth doing. Plus, I myself was kind of excited about
thowing a ball, even to a Jap wearing a Yankee cap, my
two main-most enemies right in one. I said I'd teach him
what I could.

Yoshi come shook my hand till I thought well water
was going to pour out of my mouth. The Admiral was
smiling. The kid give me a mitt and we was off to the
beanfield.

I've smelled perfume from Paris and barbeque from
Beaumont, but there ain't no better smell on God's good
earth than a well-oiled baseball glove. The mitt he give me
was a fine one, just like we used in the majors but with Jap
chickenscratch on it. It wasn't broke in good but it would
more than do. Yoshi tossed me one easy. I missed it. My
eye. With one, I just couldn't judge it—depperception, it's
called. With one eye, you got none.

I thought about the time I asked Neckless what was
the best way to catch a spitball. He said you just wait till
it quits rolling, and then you pick it up with your mitt
hand. That's about what I done for a while. Gradually I
begun to get the hang of it. It was a pure-dee joy to sling
my arm again.

Yoshi wasn't a bad ballplayer. He had a good arm; it
was just a tad short. He'd never play pro ball in the U.S.,
but he'd of been in the rotation at Smackover High. He
was likely wondering where I got off calling myself a
pitcher. I was so weak I couldn't thow a baseball through
a thick fog.

Next day my arm was so sore I couldn't hardly eat
my soup without squeaking. The palm of my left hand was

all puffed and tender. That mitt didn't appear to be as padded as I thought.

I had to do Japanese gardening till after lunch, then coach pitching till dark. Suited me. It could of been a lots worse. I could of been in the pipe, or in a Superfortress, or on the mound in Yankee stadium with the bases loaded.

It would of been downright pleasant if Curly hadn't been watching everything I done, glaring at me, glaring at Yoshi. I wondered what give him the permanent reds. Here I was a shot-down prisoner, fresh out of the pipe, one eye pert near knocked out, all thanks to the Japanese, and I was in a better humor than this fellow. But then, I wasn't short, fat, bald, ugly, lazy as Uncle Deal, and losing a war I didn't have no more sense than to start. I couldn't feel sorry for him. You can't feel sorry for somebody would kick another man while he was sleeping.

The days was long and warm. Yoshi couldn't speak English as good as his pappy, but we could get along. Mostly we talked about ball. He wanted to know everything about the majors and especially about the Yankees. He was a little hurt when I told him everbody in America hated the Yankees except for immigrants, criminals, vagrants, and such. By the look on his face, you'd have thought I was telling him there ain't no Santa Claus. But I had to do it—I couldn't let him go on thinking the Yankees was people to look up to.

I enjoyed talking baseball with the boy, but I didn't know what to say when he started asking me about the Superfortress and my bombing missions. He wanted to know had I killed anybody. I figured I had, more or less. Sort of like Neckless beat up them cab drivers, by long distance. I didn't particularly want to talk about it. Didn't much want to think about it. And I couldn't tell him I only shot Jap pilots that was shooting at me because him or his paw one surely knew some that had been killed. Chances were it wasn't by me, but they was dead anyway. And dead is dead.

I did not tell him one single secret thing, so help me God. Not that I thought he would tell anybody if I had of. I *did* let him know, not in a bragging way, that we had thousands of planes and was getting stronger by the day. And madder. This seemed to affect him. Made him sad-like, sadder than when I told him the truth about the Yankees. Maybe I ought to of let him think Japan was going to win. I don't reckon it would have hurt nothing.

One morning I was raking and my eye started itchin. Before long I could feel the drone of hundreds of 29s. They filled the sky. Like most times, I didn't see no anti-aircraft fire nor fighter resistance. In a little bit, the ground started rumbling until I thought the gravel was going to jump out the flowerbed. Smoke filled the sky a few miles off in the west. The bombers kept coming, it seemed like for a hour. After the last 29 passed over and the bombing stopped, Curly come spit on me. I wasn't bothered about it because I knew and he knew, and I *knew* he knew, that it was all over but the crying.

We didn't thow that afternoon—I don't believe Yoshi come out. The Admiral had left during the bombing, and Curly locked me in the shed. I didn't get lunch nor supper. The sky to the west glowed like steady foxfire all night. I slept good.

Yoshi left driving the Admiral's car the next morning. He didn't look old enough to me to be driving, but I figured I'd lowballed his age some because of his clean looks. I caught myself worrying about him till he come back that afternoon.

I was glad when he come out with his glove and mitt ready to thow. I had never seen a kid so sad, except maybe my own self. I felt sorry for him. Decided to give him the only thing I had. I decided to show him how to thow the gooseball. There wasn't but two people in the entire world that knew how. One was dead, killed by the Japs, and here the other one was showing a Jap kid how to thow it. Figure that. I can't. Except to tell you that it seemed like the right thing to do that afternoon.

It had always aggravated Curly to no end when Yoshi and me thowed in the afternoons. It was three hours when he couldn't bother me. The Admiral or Yoshi or both of 'em must of told him to lay off me when I was coaching. We'd fixed us up a mound, rubber, and plate, which Curly had made sure was lined up on the edge of that beanfield so he had him a shade tree to watch us out from under. Which he did mostly with his eyes closed and his mouth open. That man wouldn't of hit a lick at a snake—excepting me, of course—unless the Admiral was watching.

Yoshi had a catcher's mask and bat that we used sometimes. I wore the mask when Yoshi was thowing serious. He'd be hard to catch with a half a dozen eyes, and he was some kind of tough to catch with not but one.

That day, Yoshi was thowing hard, and he told Curly to go stand in the batter's box and hold the bat so he could practice with a man at the plate. He also told him not to swing. When Curly stepped into the box, Yoshi and me both started laughing. He stood facing the pitcher head on, all ten toes pointed at the mound. He held the bat over his head like he would a sword, like a samurai fixing to split somebody down the middle. I had seen this stance before. He whanged the bat on the plate and then raised it over his head and hollered out, "Banzai!"

I give Yoshi the sign for a curve. His didn't break sharp but was what we call a roundhouse. To the batter, it looks like it's going to hit him in the head, and then it tails away until a good one just catches the outside corner of the plate about knee high. Yoshi wound up and let her fly. Curly seen that baseball coming for his head and bailed out of the box like it was on fire, flinging the bat halfway to the mound on his way. The ball hit my mitt right over the plate. I held it right there till Curly stopped rolling so he could see why we was howling.

That got his goat. He stomped back in the box and banged on the plate to where I thought he was going to break it in pieces. I give Yoshi the sign for a fastball. Yoshi wound up and let her rip. Yoshi had told Curly not to swing, and he didn't. He chopped. But when you're a batblind catcher, a chop is as good as a swing. Ball hit me square in the mask and rocked my eyeball.

I sat down to shake it off and Yoshi come to see was I okay. Curly wasn't having none of that; he wanted to hit the ball. He handed me my mask and started poking me with the bat. Seemed to be trying to yell Yoshi back to the mound. I put on the mask and told the kid to go on and pitch.

Curly was a wild man. He was whaling away at the plate till I reckon in Tokyo they probably thought we was having a earthquake. He was yelling fit to charge a machine gun nest. Seemed like things was about to get out of hand, and maybe Yoshi ought to let Curly hit it. So I give the boy the sign for a change up, thinking even if he didn't hit it, it might be going slow enough for me to catch.

Yoshi toed the rubber. Curly, facing straight to the mound, lowered his bat slowly from over his head till it pointed at Yoshi. "Banzai!" he hollered again and raised the bat over his head. Yoshi wound up and fired the ball. It wasn't no change up. It was smoke. I dove to the left and the ball passed right between Curly's legs. It came straight on through, and I caught it, but it had evidently brushed a vital organ or two because Curly fell flat of his back and didn't wake up for ten minutes. It was a good thing, too, because it took Yoshi and me that long to quit laughing. I thought my eye was going to pop clean out again. When Curly come to, he wallowed around on the ground holding hisself for a while. Yoshi and me had to walk off so he couldn't tell how tickled we was.

We couldn't go back to the house without Curly, and Curly couldn't walk for a while, so me and Yoshi set down under the tree and had us what turned out to be a heart-to-heart talk.

I asked him what was stuck in Curly's craw. He told me Curly hadn't been in the service but a few months.

He tells me, "Yamagata is not real soldier. He does not understand war."

I'm thinking maybe I ain't a real soldier either.

He says, "For many years, Yamagata most popular comical book artist."

"That sour puss?" I say. "What kind of comics did he draw? Ones about *death* clowns?"

"Family of my father, family of Yamagata know each other long time in Tokyo, before war. My father say

Yamagatasan could draw picture to make coldest heart smile."

Seems like after Japan started losing ground, the propaganda people put him to work writing a comic book about a sword-slinging, world-dominating navy pilot. Super-Nip or like that. Curly lived in Tokyo with his wife and six kids until "big bombing fall in spring." Yoshi said a hundred thousand fires came together in a fire cyclone that turned half the city to ash. Curly—Yamagata—was at work, and when he tried to get home all he found still standing of his whole neighborhood was a black water tower.

He joined the Navy the next day. Kind of like I done after Pearl Harbor. The Admiral found out he'd enlisted and had him assigned to hisself. "My father say there is no place in war for artist," Yoshi said.

I was in that raid, Major, it was in March. They said it lasted three hours. About four hundred bombers. By the time my squadron got over Tokyo, it was so smoky we couldn't find the target. We just dropped our bombs and headed home.

I jumped the subject to baseball before Yoshi could start asking me anything about the war. Found out Yoshi had been playing baseball because his daddy wanted him to, but what he'd been thinking about was war. It was just the opposite of me. I couldn't blame him with his father being a admiral and the B29's coming over every day. But what *else* I found out was this kid wanted to be a kamikaze pilot. That stole my breath, I'll tell you that.

"You ain't old enough," I said.

"I am of eighteen years," he said.

"Aw, you can't be," I said, not believing it.

"Yes. Eighteen," he said, just quiet like that.

"Well, now," I said, "you might be old enough, but I know your paw ain't going to let you go crash yourself and die somewhere out in the Pacific Ocean."

"He is very proud. He blesses me to go."

I knew his father loved him. You could see it plain whenever the Admiral talked about this boy. This was something I could not understand. I don't believe I could really even take it in.

I know I didn't think too straight when I was eighteen, either. I could remember, though it seemed like a million years since. It's all so important when you're young, even down to what color your socks are. By this time, see, I knew what mattered. No worrying about socks anymore.

So I tried to talk him out of it. I told him jokes about kamikazes: that I heard they had some great war stories, that their parachutes was guaranteed to open on impact. Yoshi grinned, but it was sort of stiff. I wasn't getting through.

I told him I knew he had guts, but he couldn't make no difference in the war now. I told him he had a great future in pro ball, even, if he wanted it, in the U.S. majors. I told him he'd be shot down before he could reach a carrier and it'd all be a waste. I told him his father didn't want him to join up but was just being brave. I told him that with my connections, I could get him signed with the Yankees. I told him every bit of this with my very straightest face. None of it mattered.

This upset me considerable. I liked this kid. We spoke baseball. We was like teammates, almost. We was friends. Here he was, eighteen years old, with a better than average curve, and learning to thow the gooseball. The war wouldn't last forever. How come he couldn't see that all he had to do was keep his head down for another couple of years and he could write his own ticket? No, he wanted to fly a plane full of explosives into a American carrier blowing hisself and a hundred gobs he'd never met to Kingdom come. *If* he was lucky enough to make it that far. He ought to have been thinking about girls and cars and baseball, and he was thinking about death and glory.

I had to do something. When the war was finally over, I had to be able to think about all those Japanese baseball diamonds filled with folks and Yoshi thowing the gooseball amongst them. I asked Yoshi to tell his paw I needed to talk to him. Yoshi said he would, but I wasn't sure.

That evening, the Admiral come to the toolshed. He seemed a little looser than he usually was. I set on my gas can, and he set on his heels like a catcher.

He says, "Gooseball, I will never be able to thank you adequately for teaching my son to pitch like a major leaguer."

I told him never mind, that he'd done plenty by taking me out of the prison camp. Told him that place was worser than Yankee Stadium, and he smiled and looked at the ground.

He spoke soft and calm, like we was in the back of church. "The war cannot last much longer," he said. "We have sown the wind and now we reap the whirlwind."

I didn't say nothing, didn't want to rub it in—and then I wasn't exactly sure what he was getting at. When the quiet started getting to me, I told him Yoshi'd been working hard, and was coming right along. "Admiral," I said, "with my gooseball in his arsenal, Yoshi'll tear it up over here when baseball starts up again."

He looked square at me. Told me this story about how a long time ago the Japs was threatened by an invasion, and up come a divine typhoon that destroyed the invading fleet. "Gooseball," he said, "the children of this divine wind, this *kamikaze,* are trying to save our islands once more. Yoshi wishes to be part of kamikaze. I have done what I could to see that he is accepted. He will go soon."

I told him I'd been meaning to talk to him about that, and about how that kamikaze business was pretty hazardous duty. I had to try something, Major. I told the Admiral Yoshi had said—"now, not in these exact *words,* mind you," I said—that he wasn't too keen on the idea of dying right now. "I believe he'd rather be a pitcher," I said, "and he'll make a good one, too, with a little more work."

He cut me off. "Yoshi is the son of many soldiers," he said, "a soldier himself who knows there is no greater glory than to die as kamikaze."

"Admiral," I said, "I *know* you love him, same as my paw loved me. Maybe more. How can you send him off to die?"

"Did your father not send you?"

"No," I said quick, but I was thinking about it. "It was my mother," I said.

"Honor is important to us, Gooseball. I think it is to you as well. If you could have traded the rest of your life for striking out the Yankees to win the pennant, would you not have done so?"

I said no, but it didn't come out very convincing.

To tell it true, though, I might have if I'd known what the next four years was to bring. And maybe I seen a little of his point, but I knew it was wrong. I don't believe dying is a thing you ought to choose. I'd tried to choose it, and I was wrong. Even a bad life is better than none.

He stared off into space for a long time. He smiled. He asked whether I was ever scared on a bombing mission. I said a course. He asked whether I had ever decided I was going to die. I said a course, many times. Anybody that has gone to war has had to decide at some time that they were going to die. They have to so they can quit worrying about it and get on with what needs to be done. Yoshi, he tells me, is old enough he had to join the service. Once he joins, he is dead, so he might as well die in glory as a kamikaze. "It is his wish," his paw said. "It is an honorable wish."

I couldn't let it go. I give him the same reasons for not doing it I give Yoshi, leaving out the jokes, but I knew from the look in his eye that he had already buried his son. Finally, I come right out and put it to him. "If your boy is already dead, Admiral, if he ain't going to pitch anymore once he leaves here, why have we been wasting our time teaching him how?"

He says, "You have heaven after here. They play ball in your heaven, don't they? Yoshi has only now, and we have done what we can to make him happy. It has been no waste, Gooseball."

I tried to understand, but I couldn't. Still don't.

The next day, they left me in the shed. I listened to two waves of 29s about three hours apart. I wasn't figuring to see Curly—because I expected his groan was still hurting him too bad to bother with me—but I was worried when Yoshi didn't come by to thow.

Didn't see him till the next day. He come by to tell me he'd collected his one-thousandth stitch. Seems the Jap boys when they enlist get a belt and have the girls put a stitch in it till they have a thousand of them, supposed to keep the boys safe. Sounds like a custom made up by some soldier that wanted an excuse to talk to girls before he got to be the guest of honor at his own funeral. I acted like it was a stupid thing to do. I hurt his feelings.

I was up in a pear tree when Yoshi come to say goodbye. He was all stitched up and ready to go. He said they was going to teach him to fly in five days. I guess it cuts a good bit off the training when you don't have to learn how to land. He come to the bottom of my ladder.

"Honorable Gooseball, my country has called me and I must go now. You have been my friend, and I pray we meet again. You will please keep our baseball until then." He laid his ball and glove carefully down by the tree.

Instead of getting off the ladder and hugging him like I should've, I told him so long like you might the milkman and went back to pruning. I could see out the corner of my eye that he bowed to me anyway. After a few seconds, he walked away and then I heard the car. Never saw him again.

Earlier that morning, I'd been weeding in the front garden when Yoshi and the Admiral come out of the front door. The Admiral was in full uniform and wearing my mitt. Yoshi was carrying a ball and wearing his glove. They went past me without a word to me or each other, and faced off at about forty feet. They begun to thow, slow at first. The Admiral looked stiff till he worked up a little sweat. The thowing got harder and harder till each one was making a little grunt as he let the ball go. Still no talk, no smiles. This was not a friendly game of catch—this was burnout.

For ten, fifteen minutes they went at it. Then one got away from the Admiral and sailed way over Yoshi's head. Yoshi never even turned around to see where it went to. He tucked his glove under his arm, bowed to his pappy, and went back in the house. The Admiral looked at where the ball had gone for the longest time. Then he held the mitt to his face and smelled deep of it. He stared at the sun till I feared he'd go blind. Then he went back in the house, too.

Major, I can't tell you how bad I felt to see that boy go off to kill hisself. I'd have gladly took him for a little brother. He would not have hurt me for the world, and he was going to fly a Jap plane into a carrier or a destroyer or a battleship full of guys just like me. I would not hurt him neither, but I'd been out there trying my dead-level best to shoot down young Jap pilots like him and get our bombs dropped on their factories and harbors and cities. You figure.

I did not know how a father could send his boy off to die, but then didn't my mother send me? Major, I made up my mind in the Admiral's front yard that I would never send my son off to war, at least not until the Huns crossed the Mississippi.

That night, I woke up sweating and shaking. I tried to catch them babies all night long.

The next morning, Curly wasn't there to let me out of the shed. About mid-morning, I knocked the hinges off the door with a shovel. The place was deserted. The car was gone. I went into the house and helped myself to some food. I stayed put for a while, near a week I guess. It took about that long before I realized the bombers wasn't coming over no more.

The eatable food run out. Scrounging for some, I found a shortwave and made out the war was over.

15

I was glad the war was over, but I wasn't too happy it had ever started in the first place. I had lost too many things dear to me. My brother, baseball, my little buddy—and I was going back to Smackover with a pirate patch over one eye and half seeing. I should've been glad I was going home at all. Lots didn't.

I don't mind saying I kind of hated to leave the Admiral's place. I know the Army ain't looking to hear this, but to be honest I got to say my time there was probably the best I spent the whole war. It was the most like home somehow—home like I remembered it. Home like it was once.

I went down to the front gate and didn't know which way to go. I knew the prison camp was to the south. To the west and north was where the B-29's had pounded at least once a week for the past several months. I picked north. I had bundled me up some food and Yoshi's ball and glove.

I passed some women and children and some old folks, but nobody spoke. Most didn't even look, and the ones that did, stared. Not mean stares, stares like there was nothing back of their eyes. The closer I come to the city, the worse things looked, or better I guess, depending on whose side you was pulling for.

When I hadn't been walking but twenty, thirty minutes, I come to this one little village. It was poor as Job's turkey. In the middle of the crossroad was a woman, sitting on her heels like they do, holding about a four-year-old girl. As I got closer, she started calling to me like she needed help. None of the Japs was doing nothing for her. So I says what the hay and go to see what she wants. The kid she's holding don't look quite right, and when I got up to them, I seen that the kid wasn't but half a kid, nothing from the waist down. Nothing. Just air.

The mother reached for me, scared me half to death. I didn't know what to do. It made me sick. I got kindly wrought up—kindly *mad*—that the lady would be holding half a kid in the middle of a crossroads. Why didn't somebody bury it?

I started back to the Admiral's to get a shovel out of the shed, but by the time I got there, I'd talked myself into believing that the Japs didn't bury their dead no how, so why waste the time. I kept going south till I got to the prison camp.

I can still see that half a kid just as plain as anything.

I finally made contact with the Occupation Army and after some debriefing and a once-over by some Army quacks, I mean doctors, they shipped me to Okinawa, then Hawaii, then to a hospital in California. California seemed like a nice place, and I thought of settling there until I figured out I was just stalling, trying to keep from going home.

I called Dixie before I called my mother. I had to know how she had took my letter. She was so happy to hear from me she started bawling. There was a cat on the line somewhere and I couldn't hear her good so we cut it short. I told her to put a candle in the window for me. It felt good talking to her, like somebody loved me. I would go home, marry Dixie, and make a life for her and little Jackson. So long as I kept my patch on, I wasn't too terrible looking. I didn't seem to frighten American children. Dixie could do worse for herself.

On the train going home I planned out everything. I had planned it out once before back in the prison camp hospital, but then it was more a wish. Now I was really going home. Everything was going to be okay. Shoot, everything was going to be great.

It was a Sunday morning in November. Maybe the finest day ever in the history of the world, who knows. Barning time. I walked from the bus station to Dixie's folks' house. Passed my house right by. Besides wanting Dixie to be the first person I seen, I knew Maw would want to look under my eyepatch and ask me all kind of questions I didn't care about answering.

Once I rung the bell at Dixie's, I almost run away. I didn't, but no one come. Maybe they was at church. I figured I'd go see Maw.

The old house hadn't changed much. Maw had done a good job keeping it up. Especially by herself. I knocked, and Dixie opened the door. She was even more fetching than I had remembered. Pretty as a movie star. Plumb beautiful.

Anyway, she thowed her arms around me and went to crying. I nearly did, too, thinking about Jugs. He should have been the one coming back.

While we was hanging on to each other, here come little Jackson. Looked just like Jugs. Ears like little jug handles. Even had what was left of a shiner. He hadn't never seen me that he could remember, but he took to me right off. I picked him up and give him a great big old hug. He wasn't one to be tied down, so he kicked me in the groan in a playful way.

Then here come Maw, big as a heifer and squawling like a orphan calf. She hugged me and kissed me. The thing I noticed was how she smelled. She'd smelled the same since I could remember, of this lavender bath powder she kept in an old-timey box. It was good to be home.

Then come Jude. He was dressed in a suit, and had a little Clark Gable mustache under his nose—looked like he'd been drinking chocolate milk. But you seen him. He had a smirk on his face fit for a second looey, meaning no disrespect, sir.

He says to Dixie out the side of his mouth while he's looking at me, "Well, Dixie, Jackson makes it unanimous. You appear to be the Fielders' choice."

"Jude," I told him, "I quit playing games a long time ago. You got something to say, you better say it."

"Three's a crowd, Jax," he said.

I didn't get it, but I didn't like his attitude. "Come on, let's go out on the front porch, little brother, and I'll show you a one-man crowd."

Then he says, real smart, "We got your letter. The one where you asked Dixie to marry you."

What was he doing reading my letter, I'm thinking. I looked at her. She didn't look up; she was still crying. He laughed and said they was sorry but that he had married Dixie in June. Dixie said nothing. I said nothing. My ears was ringing. Maw come over, hugged me, and tried to look under my patch. I walked out.

I wound up at the ballfield, there at the old water tower. I climbed the ladder and looked over the town. It was the same place but a different time. I spent the rest of the morning spitting off the tower, thinking about how it would feel to dive off. I knew how it would feel on the way down; I just didn't know how it would feel to hit.

About noon, I seen the El Dorado bus heading to the station. I had my money in my pocket, and I climbed down off the tower and caught the bus to St. Louis.

Baseball season had been over for more than a month, but I decided to go by the front office just to see maybe if anybody remembered me. Connie White was there and I think he really was glad to see me. Said he'd heard I was killed in the Pacific. I reckon since he thought I was dead and gone, he'd forgiven me for losing the pennant in '41. At least for the time being.

We sat in the office there and chewed the fat all afternoon. We talked about players that was killed or maimed in the war and others that had got to play—and even won the pennant for him in '44—who couldn't have mowed the grass much less hit a loud foul in a major league park if the rest of us hadn't been off fighting.

"How did you do it?" I asked him.

He looked at me, peaceful as a preacher, and said, "All those years, I was looking for steel-eyed killers, and we

won the pennant with a bunch of 4-Fs that had nothing
but heart."

"So you ain't still looking for a magician," I said to
him, half as a joke.

"I'd rather have a good kid with a trick or two up his
sleeve," he said.

We went on, laughing and remembering some of the
stunts folks pulled off that year I played for him.

He got around to asking about my eye—asked me
how I lost it. I said I didn't exactly lose it, it just got
lowered a notch.

"How old are you now, Gooseball?" he asks me.

I says twenty-three.

"You think you can still pitch?"

I told him I thought I could be ready for next season.
I didn't really know, but that's what I said.

He asked me where I was staying, which I didn't
know, and he told me where to get a cheap room. He
wanted me to stay over and see the team doctor the next
day. He didn't say it, but he give me the idea that if my
eye was fixable, he might give me a tryout.

I couldn't hardly get to sleep that night. A jukebox
was playing "Take The A Train" over and over, and I was
pitching games again in my head all night. And I was going
to be better than ever because I was older and wiser. I
wouldn't choke again ever. I was a veteran. I had all the
magic I needed.

The next day I was in a doctor's office, not the team
doctor but a specialist surgeon. Mr. White said what he
did was rebuild faces, and the war had give him lots of
practice. He was a Browns fan and was doing this as a favor
to Mr. White.

He examined me for a long time—looked in my eyes, took a bunch of pictures, took a imprint of my good side, and then sent me away and told me he'd make a report to Mr. White. I took this as a bad sign. Figured he didn't have the heart to look me in the eye and tell me I was through.

I hung around the front office for two days. Since the doctor wasn't charging, Mr. White didn't feel right rushing him. I mostly sat in Mr. White's office listening to him talk on the phone about how many minor leaguers he'd had to field the last season and how he was hoping to run down some good ballplayers coming back from the war. I guess the war years was hard on everybody, even old Mr. White.

On the third day, a kid come over with the report from the doc. It went three pages. Said I was in good shape except for signs of malnutrition, but my crushed cheekbone was causing my eye to drop and me to see double. The doctor said he could operate on me and put in a plastic cheek and reset my eyeball.

Mr. White read the report out loud to me. It finished up saying the operation would cost one thousand dollars. My heart sunk at that kind of money. Coach asked me what I thought. I told him I wanted to play ball again. He took off his cap and rubbed his bald head, all the time staring at the report. Finally he said he was willing to take a chance on me. The Browns would pay to fix my eye if I'd agree to play one season, majors or minors, for room and board. I didn't even need to think on it. I was going to play ball again.

The Doc wasn't friendly, and he had a big red nose didn't come from drinking buttermilk, but I reckon he knew what he was doing. When he finally took off the bandage, I could see all right. My eyes was back on track. He went in through the same scars so it wouldn't look no worse, but you can see it still looks a little bit like the top of a old basketball shoe without the laces. The plastic cheek has took good so far.

Maw, Dixie, and little Jackson come to see me in the hospital. I had said for them not to, but they did. I had a hard time looking at Dixie. I don't know if I was more embarrassed about my face or about the letter I had wrote her out of the blue, asking her, or more like *telling* her to marry me when I come home. And there she was already married to my little brother. She didn't say nothing about it, which was nice of her.

Little Jackson was into everything. He was five and had already knocked his front teeth out. All boy and a yard wide. Like his pappy.

Maw wanted me to come back and work at the furniture store for Uncle Woodley and Jude. She couldn't understand why I would even think about playing baseball again. She said, "But you're all growed now, son. Baseball's a boys' game." I think Dixie understood. She said it would be swell to listen to the games again on the radio with me pitching. She knew what a dream means to a person.

I went on home to Smackover after I got out of the hospital. I needed to put on twenty or thirty pounds before reporting to battery camp in March. It was nice living and eating with Maw again and sleeping in my own room. Early mornings, I did some roadwork to try to build up a appetite. I'd force down a dozen or so cathead biscuits with lots of sorghum, but I couldn't seem to put on no weight.

Jude give me a job delivering furniture and sweeping the warehouse, and I appreciated it. He had got to be a big shot since I left. Stayed out of the war by being 4-F on account of his back. I believe what's wrong is it's got a bad yellow streak.

He is something. God Almighty's overcoat wouldn't make him a vest. He claims to be well thought of as a businessman even though he is a pup and slick as a button. Took Maw's insurance money from Paw dying and has bought up rent houses in Smackover and El Dorado with the idea of sticking it to the GIs when they come home looking for a place to live. Like a tick getting fat off a hardworking dog.

Still, it was pretty good being home. Big Mr. Houston Texas, old Bubba Broadax who'd caught me my senior year, he was the head deputy sheriff. I talked to him, or tried to, for a second at the drugstore the day I got back. I couldn't tell if he was still mad at me for the melon thing. He wouldn't say much, but he still had that look in his eye.

16

I saw Dixie and little Jackson almost ever day, either at the furniture store or at our house. Seeing her was the best and worst part of my day—best because she was so nice and good to talk to, worst because my heart hurt when I *did* talk to her and kept hurting long after. I don't know why I felt so bad. It's not like I'd lost her; you can't lose what you never had. Probably I was just embarrassed.

Coach let me in the gym to thow at night and on the weekends. Usually I could find a high school kid to thow with. If not, I'd pitch my same old rubber ball against the wall. When I first started, the kids I drafted thew harder than me. It was after New Year's before I started trying to really put her out there. Even when I tried, it wasn't much use at first. Little by little, my arm has come around. Now it's feeling fine as frog hair.

Mr. White called ever Sunday night from St. Louis to see how I was doing. I'd give it to him straight, but he was always encouraging. Whatever it took, I was going to pitch in the bigs again or die trying.

Last month, the night before I was scheduled to leave for battery camp in Tucson, Maw and Dixie thew a regular go-and-come for me. Dixie's folks was there, and neighbors and friends. Jude come a few hours late. Said he had some important legal business. Dixie was peeved but didn't say anything to him. She never said much to him at all, and what she did say was always in a civil tongue but not what you'd call loving.

Folks had passed the hat and got me a big old travel trunk. It was nice and beat my GI duffel bag all hollow. Jackson had a big time clambering all over it. It was might near big enough for him to do chinups on the bar.

Later on, when the party was winding down and the women was cleaning up, little Jackson come in with a couple of knobs he'd pulled off of Maw's radio. I didn't think nothing of it, and I'm sure Maw didn't. But as soon as Jude seen them knobs, he whipped off his belt, saying "I told you, now didn't I tell you," while he doubled it up, and quick as that, he backhanded little Jackson about neck high.

It took me a second or two to believe what I was seeing, but then I come out of my chair, saying, "Whoa, now!" Little Jackson wasn't crying. He was just staring up at Jude and rubbing his little neck. Jude swung at him again but Jackson caught most of it on his arm.

Everybody was froze. I got in between 'em and bent down over little Jackson. He had an angry red whelp around his neck. Then Jude swatted me with his belt on my back.

"Get out the way, Jax. This isn't your concern," he said.

I raised up and turned around real slow. The neighbors and all backpedalled like you see 'em do in a western before a gunfight.

"Little Jackson is *my* son, and I will discipline him," he started to say.

Before he could finish, I had grabbed him around the Adam's apple and lifted him up on his toes. I told him Jackson was *not* his son, he was Jugs's son and my nephew, and if I ever heard about him hitting little Jackson again, I'd kill him graveyard dead. I said it like I was half crazy and I pert near was. I think he believed me. Leastways he gurgled like he did.

The party broke up fast after that. Jude was the first to leave. It had started raining hard and the guests had used that as a good excuse to hightail it home. I went back to my room as soon as I sociably could.

Dixie was there sitting on Jugs's bed, crying.

She said she wished he was still alive.

I said I did, too.

In a minute, she quit crying and we just sat there, me on my bed, her on Jugs's, listening to the rain.

"You know," she said, nodding toward the window, "this reminds me of the Night of the Grinning Killer Frog."

I busted out laughing, and so did she.

That summer before Paw died, the three of us really had us a fine time. Jugs was working at the furniture store and bought him a car. It wasn't much but it would run good. When Jugs and me wasn't playing ball, the three of us was in that car. We'd drive to El Dorado, or if we was short on gas money, we'd coast. Sometimes we'd just park and listen to the Browns games on the radio.

Jugs was always up to something. One Sunday night, we was driving out in the country, letting the car steer itself, going nowhere in particular, when Jugs skidded the car to a stop sideways in the road. He jumped out and ran. I seen him take his shirt off and thow it on top of what I guessed was some kind of animal.

Dixie and I was both in the front seat wondering what was going on when he come running back to the car holding this bundle in his arms like a baby. He put it on Dixie's lap and we took off again. The bundle was wiggling and Dixie shoved it over to me. "What is it?" I says. I thought it was a rabbit. "You ain't going to believe it. Take a look." he says.

Now, I have personally met about every type animal, bird, or fish that lives in South Arkansas. Probably kept half of them as pets, and half of those I kept probably slept in my bed till Jude told Paw on me. I ain't above getting squeamish, like when I thought Bubba's brains had splattered us or when I found that kitten eat up with maggots, but I have never been afraid of animals. I peeled back Jugs's shirt, and I liked to fainted. Reckon I might have if Dixie hadn't screamed right in my ear and kicked me in the face jumping into the back seat.

I had seen frogs. I had caught frogs. I had carried frogs in my pocket. Once, on a bet, I had kept a live tree frog in my mouth for a hour. And I know for a fact frogs got no teeth nor claws and are generally peaceable creatures. But *this* frog, this frog sitting on my *lap*, was so big and so ugly he could have treed a dog, and—may the Lord strike me dead if I'm lying—he was grinning.

My blood run cold, and I scraped my shin on the ceiling light joining Dixie in the back seat. Jugs was howling. He finally had to wrap the frog up and put it down under his side of the seat so he'd have somebody to talk to.

He took this frog to the diner and showed everybody there. He brought it by the movie theater and showed it to everybody coming out that we could coax over to the car. He took it by our house and Dixie's folks' house. Everybody agreed—right quick, so Jugs'd move on—that it was the biggest, ugliest, grinningest frog they'd ever seen. One fellow suggested we formaldehyde it and send it to the University of Arkansas for them to put in the museum. Jugs had another idea.

We went out to Rosie's Lake where folks went when they had some spooning to do. On any summer's night, there'd be six or seven cars lined up along the north shore, and the rain didn't make a whit of difference. Jugs parked off a hundred yards or so and said, "Come on, ya'll." He got out and stuck the frog, still bundled up in his shirt, under his arm like a football. Neither Dixie nor me got too close. We shared an umbrella and a natural fear of giant, smiling frogs.

We stopped about thirty yards from the parked cars, and was surprised to see Jugs walk right between two of them and down towards the lake. When he got to the water, he bent down, and I thought he might be letting the frog loose. Should have known better. All it was was an excuse to get heading the other way. He broke into kind of a lazy trot back toward us, and when he got up even with the cars, he made a perfect lateral of that frog into the driver's window of one. Since the window was about three-quarters of the way up because of the rain, it was a pretty good shot with a slick amphibian.

He come running past us about ninety-one miles a hour, and Dixie and me tailed in his wake back to the car. A couple of steps along, we heard the awfullest scream I ever did hear, even in the war, and it was not the lady. It was the scream of a grown man. Would've made Johnny Weissmuller hisself drop off the vine. One second later, the woman joined in.

Well, Dixie and me was laughing so hard we couldn't hardly stand up, much less run. By the time we made it back to the car, and told it to each other, and hooted some more, Jugs was ready to drive by and survey the damage. When we got to the lake, we seen half a dozen men standing in the pouring rain around the parked car. All its doors was open, and the men was giving its insides a careful inspection with flashlights. One of them had a shotgun, two had crowbars, and they all looked ready to use them. The women were in a big knot over a ways, comforting one that was still sort of shrieking at a low level. I don't know what happened to the poor frog. We laughed and told that story the rest of the summer—would have told it for years if we'd been there, Jugs and me.

Dixie and me needed a good laugh that night.

It was nice sitting there with her. Maybe I shouldn't have, but I asked her how she come to marry my two brothers.

She said since before she could remember, her whole life had been planned out, from where she would go to college to how many kids she was going to have and what to name them. She and Jugs had been sweet on each other for years, but he wasn't in the plan.

Then she went off to school at Fayetteville and found out somebody had forgot to tell the rest of the world about her plans, and she was lost. She was upset one night because she didn't get in some club, and Jugs happened to call her. He listened, and then he told her the fighting in Europe started when they wouldn't let Hitler into some club.

He made her feel silly. He made her laugh. Told her he was going to rescue her from the horrible slow death of a regular housewife. And not so much by what he said, but by how he lived, he talked her into living life with him, one day at a time, no plan.

She said when she found out Jugs was missing and presumed dead, she told herself he'd come back. She told herself nothing could kill him. She imagined him playing a joke on his buddies somehow. Even at the service, with all the weeping, in the back of her heart she kept the candle burning.

It wasn't until she borrowed Jude's new car one Saturday to drive to Shreveport by herself to do some shopping that it finally hit her. She was coming home at dusk on old Highway 77 out in the middle of nowhere when a pack of razorbacks come across the road. She stomped the brakes, but she hit about three of them, killing one clean. Two of them lay in the road squealing, bleeding, guts and eyeballs knocked out. One was a mama because a litter of about ten little pigs went to squawling after her. Dixie rolled up the windows and turned up the radio but it couldn't shut out the sound. The grill was caved in and both lights was broke so she couldn't drive on, even if she could have weaved her way through the ham. She sat there for a couple of hours before a truck driver come along and give her a ride to Smackover.

She said that as she sat in the dark car and the squealing of the hogs stopped as they died, and the squawling of the little pigs settled down as they seen their mama wasn't getting up, she knew Jugs was dead. And there she was without Jugs and without a plan. She said she cried long after the little pigs had give up and disappeared into the woods.

Jude had been making proposals to her of one sort or another since Jugs's service. He made her feel pretty bad about wrecking his car, guilty enough, she said, that she didn't hold him off no longer. Seemed to me a wrecked car wasn't enough reason; I reckon she was worn out and scared and didn't know what else to do. Then I come up missing and presumed dead. After that, she said, she felt so bad she figured she was just getting what she deserved. If it wasn't for little Jackson, she would have killed herself long before then. I wanted to put my arms around her and tell her it was all right.

There was a crashing of plates in the kitchen and we both knew little Jackson was on the prowl again. She had to go. She turned around as she was leaving and told me it almost killed her when she thought I was dead, too. I said it wasn't no picnic for me neither and tried to laugh. After she left, I strangled my pillow.

17

Gooseball. It had been a while since anybody but the Admiral and Yoshi had called me that. It felt good. It would've felt great except I didn't have much of a gooseball. I wasn't strong enough...yet. I had a slow curve, a change up, and the thing I used to call my fastball.

Besides the pitchers and catchers, the rookies was in camp. They looked like babies to me, like the high school kids I was thowing in the gym with a few days before. I don't know if the kids never heard of me or what, but no one give me the business about the big boner. Maybe it was my scar. Maybe it was because I still looked a little bit like I had been thawed out from the Lazy Lizard Dude Ranch. I don't know.

I'd been in camp about two weeks when Jude called and said he urgently needed to speak with me. I asked if something was wrong with Maw again.

Maw had give us a scare right after last Christmas. Since Paw left, and especially after Jugs died, she had took to eating for a hobby and had got even bigger. One night she waked me up out of a dead sleep calling for me to come quick. I went in her room and there she was, piled up with pillows and blankets, having a lot of trouble breathing. She said she was having a heart attack, but she didn't want me to get no doctor. She wanted me to go get Jude so he'd be there when she passed. I called the doctor anyway, and once I was sure he was on the way, I called Jude.

Jude had knocked the phone off the hook so I couldn't call him back, and I had to run down the street to his house to get him. I told them Maw was having a heart attack and the whole family come running, Dixie toting little Jackson.

We all got there huffing and puffing and circled round Maw's bed. Things looked bad. She was heaving up and down and moaning like a alley cat. She tried to talk but she couldn't. Me and Dixie looked at one another, not knowing what to do nor think. Jude started whimpering. It seemed like it took the doctor forever to get there.

When the doctor finally showed up, we was all fraught. He took out his headphones and started listening to Maw's heart. The room was deathly still. All of a sudden the doc jumped back like he had been shocked with a live wire. Then there was a sound like I never heard before nor since. Close as I can describe it is that it sounded somewhere between a cow's moo and a train whistle. What it was was a five-second burp.

This time, Dixie and me didn't look at each other, because if we had, it would have been all over. Maw sat up and said she felt just fine now. The doctor stuck his headphones back in his bag, give me a glare, and left without a word. I went back to bed. Dixie stayed to get Maw a piece of pecan pie.

Jude said no, Maw was still fat and happy. But he wanted me to come home right then. I asked him what was up. He wouldn't say, other than there was a scandal brewing and it had to do with me. I told him I didn't care about no scandal, I was a ballplayer, not a movie star, and I hung up on him.

Turns out, he was just coursing the bee to the hive.

Two weekends ago, Jude showed up at camp in Arizona. He come got me off the field. Said it was "a matter of life and death." I reckoned he wasn't going to let me be, so I went back to the clubhouse with him. He was all nervous and fidgety. I asked him how little Jackson was just to let him know I hadn't forgot our last meeting.

He jumped right on into what had brung him. He said he had come to warn me. Said two Army investigators had come by asking all kind of questions, like whether I had ever wrote or got letters from Japan before, during, or after the war. They went through my room like mice going through a breadbox, turning over every crumb. They was asking the neighbors about me, too. A course, Jude said, he *had* to tell 'em where I was and that I *had* been acting a little strange since coming home from Japan. Lord only knows what else he lied about.

I didn't have too many fond memories of the service, and I didn't give a hang about how the Army spent its time. I told him to go on home and tell the Army whatever he pleased. Said that unless they was to draft me, find me, catch me, and hogtie and brand me, me and the Army wasn't going to do no more business together.

Jude says this has all become a terrible scandal in Smackover, and Maw is hurt and embarrassed by it. Says Dixie is shocked, and they both hope little Jackson never finds out what it was I done overseas. All at once I could tell what he really wanted. It was killing him: he didn't know enough about what happened to be able to do me serious damage.

"Jax," he says, "I'm your brother, your only brother. We Fielders have to stick together in the tough times. You've got to tell me what this is about so I can help you."

I asked him if he could keep a secret. He swore on everybody's grave we ever knew.

I told him, "I don't really *know* what happened. All I remember is on Tinian I would get these terrible headaches, and there was this tail-gunner kept asking me all the time what was wrong. I told him to mind his own business, but he kept bothering me, and the more he bothered me, the more my head hurt. Then one day they found him...or what was left of him. At first they said he must have fell from thirty thousand feet, he was so flat. But then they found a bloody pipe under my bed, and now they think I done it. Me," I said, "I don't remember a thing, Jude."

I don't know which was open wider, his eyes or his mouth. I started rubbing my head and saying, "I just don't remember, I don't remember, I just don't remember." Then I looked over at the bat rack sitting right there, and Jude followed my eyes. He headed for the door, saying he'd call me.

I said like I was crying, "Don't go, Jude, you're the only friend I got!" Next thing I heard was his new Nash spraying gravel. I probably should have ended that conversation by popping his head like a melon, but I just walked out of the clubhouse and back to practice.

I wondered what all *was* going on, but I wasn't going to lose no sleep over it. No offense, Major, but I knew the

Army well enough to know they don't need a good reason to do whatever they do. They was probably hunting Japanese souvenirs to confiscate, of which I took back none except for this scar which they are welcome to.

It was last week, the day before our first exhibition game, I was called into Mr. White's office. There was a man with him that he introduced to me as the team lawyer. Had a Clark Gable mustache like Jude's. The lawyer said the Army had contacted the team to let them know I was under suspicion of "having aided and abetted" the Japanese Army while I was a prisoner of war in Japan. I didn't get it at first—kind of hard to aid and abet from inside a pipe—and the lawyer explained that the Army was accusing me of being a traitor.

The bottom line was, the Browns couldn't afford to have a traitor, nor even somebody *accused* of being a traitor, on the team. He said I could cause the Browns to lose their franchise.

I couldn't believe it. Sure, I thowed the baseball with a Jap boy, but I don't see how that aided the enemy unless we was planning to play Japan a seven-game series for the Pacific. Which probably would have been a better idea.

I looked at Mr. White. He had always been more than fair to me, and I knew he was as independent as a pig on ice. He said it wasn't his decision. Said he knew I wasn't a traitor and he hoped everything worked out, but management has decided that until I clear my name, I am suspended without pay, which for me means without room and board.

The team lawyer said not to talk to nobody until I got myself my own lawyer. He said the Department of the Army was coordinating with the Department of Justice, and they was going to have some sort of board of inquiry and maybe court martial me.

The lawyer talked at me for near a hour, but after the first few minutes, I quit listening. All I could think about was Yoshi. What a good kid. What a waste. I wish he was still alive so he could tell them how I aided the enemy. I wish I had told him good-bye.

I cleaned out my locker and Mr. White give me a bus ticket back to Smackover. He said they'd passed the hat for it. I think he sprung for it hisself.

Nobody asked me why I was leaving, so I guess word had got around fast.

It was the same in Smackover. Nobody asked me why I was back, so I knew they'd heard something—more than likely from my brother—but I just didn't know what exactly. Maw was pretending hadn't nothing happened, and Jude kept Dixie and little Jackson clear of me.

Poor little Jackson. I feel bad about Jackson, Major. Feel like what happened to him last night was my fault.

A few days ago, two Army investigators come by my house to talk to me. They told me they wanted to help me. I right away reached to make sure my wallet was still in my pocket. They said they knew everything about what I'd done after being released from the prison camp in Japan, and they just wanted me to clear up some details. I said okay.

The first thing they read said on or about June such and such until the end of the war, I "met with and advised Admiral Yamama about American aircraft strength, American bombing targets," and a flock of other things they called "vital to the war effort and of a highly classified nature." I got so mad when they was reading that pigswill that I almost thowed them out of my house by the nape of the neck. Instead, I nicely told them to go pound sand down a rat hole. Had I knew I was still technically in the Army, I'd have said, "rat hole, sir." They acted all surprised and insulted that I would be upset and told me to call them when I felt more "cooperative".

That night I called Mr. White. I told him I had been thinking about Mexico and I didn't want to miss the season. He didn't ask nothing, just said if I could get back to Tucson before camp broke this weekend, he'd make sure I got to Mexico to play ball. I told him I'd be there as soon as I could.

I had decided there wasn't much use to fight something I knew wasn't true. I didn't ask for the war to happen. I went and dropped bombs and shot down Zeroes like I was sposed to. I didn't ask to be sent to no prison camp or to be took in by no Jap admiral. All I ever wanted to do was play baseball. If what I done was a federal crime, then let it be one. They played ball in other places, and other places was fine with me.

I packed the trunk my neighbors had give me when we was still on speaking terms. Before I left, I went down to the high school to watch the team work out. While I was there, Bubba come out to the field with an M.P. who give me orders to come see you here today. Bubba didn't say nothing, but I got the feeling he kindly enjoyed that part of his job. Before he walked off, he shaded his eyes and looked up at the water tower. He still had that look.

I didn't even hardly know what a court martial was before yesterday, and I still ain't too sure, but I knew enough to know I didn't want no part of it. I was going to Mexico.

When I got back to the house around supper time last night, Jude was waiting. Maw had seen my trunk packed and sent for him. He tells me I can't leave town because I'd been issued some orders. I ask him how *he* knows I got orders. He said Maw told him, which wasn't a too-smart lie because I hadn't told her.

He followed me back into my room and stood between me and the door. He told me how I can't run away from this problem, that a traitor could never have a country, *any* country. He said I always run from my problems. I told him maybe so, but I never run from him and I'd just as soon go through him as around him.

He said I had to stop running and pay my debt to society. I said I already done that in a pipe in Japan. He didn't know what I was talking about, but that never slowed him down. He said he'd talked to the Army and they'd talked to the Department of Justice and that if I just pleaded no contest—not "guilty," just "no contest"—they'd see I didn't get no longer than five years in prison.

I asked him who made him my lawyer, and he said he was just protecting the good name of his dead father and his dead brother and his son that had been named after me and would have to live the rest of his life with whatever I decided. I told him to go ride a razorback and he left.

The thing that really got to me was him saying I was a quitter. No one ever called me that before. Maybe I was one.

But it wasn't no use to do different, Major. How was anyone going to believe that I just happened to meet up with a fan of mine in Japan that just happened to be a Jap admiral who wore a Yankees cap and kept me in a toolshed and got me to teach his boy how to thow my gooseball?

Americans, present company expected, think all Japs are yellow-skinned, slant-eyed devils who can't think of nothing but crashing their planes into California school-houses. Americans don't know that Japanese have kids and love their kids and play catch with them and tote them to little league practice. I wouldn't believe it myself if I hadn't seen it with my own eyes. Maybe I was running away again, but if I was, it was for the last time. When I got to Mexico, that was it.

Besides saying goodbye to Maw, I had to go see Dixie and little Jackson before I left. With me leaving maybe for keeps, I needed to give him something to remember me by. I had a baseball that was sort of autographed by Babe Ruth that I was sure he'd like when he got a little bigger. I say "sort of" because it might've been, but then again it mightn't have.

Neckless had what he swore to be a ball autographed by Babe Ruth when Neckless met him in Memphis in 1938 at a exhibition game. Players around the league knew Neckless had the ball and they was always trying to buy it off him. One rainout, somebody, not me, had the idea to make Neckless some money by selling the ball. Because there was more buyers than balls, we borrowed several dozen balls from the clubhouse and started copying Babe Ruth's autograph on all of 'em. So we wouldn't exactly cheat nobody, we thowed the real ball in the bag with the copies. That way, when you swore it was truly signed by Ruth, you wasn't altogether lying. That was my idea. It sounds worse telling it to you than it did doing it. I didn't make no money off the deal, but I did get to pick a ball out the bag. I don't know if it was the real ball or not, but it wasn't one I had signed, because I used a blue pen.

I walked down the corner to Jude and Dixie's house and knocked. Nobody come. I knocked again. I could hear racket in the back of the house, so I knew they was home. Jude finally opened the door all red in the face and out of breath. I told him I'd come to tell Dixie and Jackson so long.

Right off, he started yelling at me and the rest of the county, saying I couldn't leave town, I was under investigation by the U.S. Government; said he hadn't believed I was a traitor but me running away proved I was; said that he hisself was calling the law to stop my craven escape. Then he slammed the door in my face and locked it.

I started to kick the door in and mop the floor with him for old times sake, but all of a sudden I got scared. Not of Jude, but of Jude calling the law—which meant Bubba. Bubba had that look like he wouldn't mind getting even for the melon that white-eyed him such a long time ago. And after my life lately, I did not want to spend one more second in a jail of any kind. I made a lot of promises to me and to God while I was in that pipe, but the main-most one to us both was that nobody would ever lock this cracker up again. This one I will keep, no disrespect intended, sir.

I decided to take to the backyards to get home. I come around the corner of Jude's house and heard a kid squealing and feet scuffling on the raised hardwood floors. Through the blinds—which was mostly closed—I could see Jude whupping little Jackson. Over and over with a belt. I could hear Dixie telling him to stop, but he wouldn't. I yelled as loud as I could and kicked the side of the house so hard the screens rattled. The beating stopped. Jude come to the window and pulled down a section of the blinds to see through. I'll never as long as I live and breathe forget his face. His eyes was red and wild and he was breathing like a cornered horse. It was the devil hisself.

Part of me wanted to run, but I was froze there looking at him. It wasn't until he let go of the blind slats and turned away from the window that I could move my legs.

I turned for home, and then I said, wait a minute. What am I doing? I'm leaving Jugs's little boy and sweet wife to the devil. They was the only people left on this earth that meant anything to me, even though they weren't mine.

I knew a man once that sent his boy off to a sure and certain death instead of fighting tradition for him. I always knew that deep down, no matter how many reasons he give himself, the Admiral knew he killed that boy same as if he'd tied him in a towsack and thowed him in a river. Same result. I knew that if I left Little Jackson right then, he'd have a life worse than death. Same result. I was not going to drop no more babies. I was going to stop Jude, once and for all.

I took off back around the corner of the house at full tilt. I jumped the front porch rail and hit the door on the fly just as Jude got there. I busted in the door and knocked Jude back about fifteen feet into the chiffarobe in the hall. Him and his shotgun. He come up fast and drew down on me with Uncle Woodley's old pump.

That sight and the sound of tires locking up in the gravel behind me froze me again in the doorway. I never turned around nor took my eyes off Jude. I recognized it was Bubba yelling, "Whoa! Whoa!" behind me. He come halfway up the walk at a gallop with his shotgun before he seen what was happening. He froze, too, making it unanimous.

"What's going on here, boys?" he says, trying to sound like he'd caught two kids smoking behind the gym. But he could see Jude's face, and he knew this wasn't just a brotherly spat.

"What's going on, Jax?" he says to me.

"I got to kill him," I says, slow and dead serious.

"Oh, great!" I hear him say to hisself. "Why don't you tell me what this is all about, Jude?" he yells.

Jude says he's keeping me from escaping. He said I'd gone berserk and was threatening to kill him and his family. Bubba told him not to get his panties in a bunch and asked him to put his shotgun down. Jude says he's got a legal right to protect his family. Bubba tells him to put the gun down and Jude lowers it from his eye. Bubba tells me to back off the porch. I didn't move. As long as I was between Jude and Bubba, neither of them would shoot at me.

Then come a pitter-patter out of the back of the house. Jude took a swipe at little Jackson with the butt of his shotgun, trying to stop him as he come flying out of his room and turned for the front door. I heard Bubba pump his shotgun. I stiffened my neck and waited for the pellets. The gun butt knocked little Jackson down, but he got right up and headed for me. Jude raised his gun again, this time pointed at little Jackson's back. Little Jackson seemed like he was running in slow motion. I caught a glimpse of Dixie in the bedroom door. I never thought about it, but in one motion, I went down to grab little Jackson and slung the Babe Ruth autographed baseball gooseball-style at Jude, hitting him about chest high and knocking him on his behind. I swallowed up little Jackson and rolled out of the doorway leaving Bubba and Jude squared off.

Little Jackson wasn't crying, but he had a right to. Even in the porch light, I could see he had a shiner and a busted lip. He clung to me tight as a pea vine on a picket fence, but he squirmed when I held him because of the whelps on his legs.

Bubba seen it the same time as me. "Who did this to you, son?" he asked real soft.

"Jax! Jax hit him. He's crazy!" says Jude.

"Jax nothing. I asked the boy!" Bubba snapped out. By the way he said it, I knew he knew. He was just gathering evidence. Little Jackson buried his head into my shoulder.

"It was Jude," Dixie said. She finally came out of the bedroom.

Jude cut his eyes at the shotgun laying beside him. Bubba seen it and said, "Do us all a favor, Jude, and reach for that shotgun."

Jude hung his head. He wasn't sorry; he had just lost.

Dixie walked past Jude and took little Jackson from me.

Bubba said, "Jude Fielder, I've got a good mind to let your brother here finish what he started. But I don't want to see him in no more trouble than he is now. But *you*, you look me dead in the eye and hear that I'm telling you the gospel. If I ever see you in Smackover or even hear you're in this part of Arkansas, I'll arrest you for child beating and make sure you spend a long time in jail. That is, if your brother don't kill you first, which I won't arrest him for if he does. Do you understand? I'll give you five minutes to pack what you can and get out of here."

He was gone in four.

I took Jackson and Dixie back to Maw's. I knew Bubba had converted Jude, but I also knew Jude was crazy and mean as a striped snake. I didn't want to take chances.

I told Maw as much as I thought she'd listen to about her favorite son, her baby. She said Jude was just sensitive and we didn't understand him. Said Jugs and me had teased him till he was mean, so it was our fault. She told Dixie she should get down on her knees and kiss his feet for giving her and little Jackson a home when no one else would.

"Maw," I said to her, "all that's fine and I ain't going to argue with you about it, but I'll tell you one thing that should've been on the tablets give to Moses: You might have problems, but when you hurt a child on purpose you have crossed the line and should be smote down by any bystander or passerby, with less thought than you'd give to smashing a mosquito on the back of your hand."

We left and spent the night over to Dixie's folks. They didn't ask us what happened. But you did, Major, and that's the whole truth.

18

Look at my hands, Major. They been shaking like this since my first mission over Japan. I was a nineteen-year-old professional athlete when I enlisted in nineteen and forty-one. Five years later, I got the body of a seventy-year-old man. I can't afford to spend one more day locked up. I won't.

I've decided on where I want to go from here, but the Army and baseball got trump cards. So now you've got to make a decision for the Army, and I reckon the new commissioner's got to make one for baseball. I hope you don't judge me on my life, because I have made some bad decisions. I admit it. And I hope you don't judge me on my decisions, either, good or bad, because I ain't always had control over how they turned out. I ask that you judge me on whether I done what I done for the right reasons. That's all I ask.

Last fall when me and Connie White was holed up in his office waiting for the doctor to decide whether he could realign my headlights, he told me how the Browns won the pennant in forty-four. It wasn't what you'd expect, especially if you knew the crusty old bird. The only thing he wanted in his life was to win a pennant. He wanted it so bad it controlled every thought he had. He said that, in a way, he'd sold his soul to the devil long ago trying to get that flag, because he hadn't done a good deed in fifty years unless he thought it might get him closer to it. When all us good players left to go fight, he figured he'd never get a pennant, and he got even meaner.

Then come Jeffrey. Jeffrey was a simpleton that loved everything, but mostly St. Louis Browns baseball. He started showing up outside the players' gate before and after the games just to see the players come out. For the first month of the season, he didn't speak even when the players would say something to him. One afternoon after a game, he tried to talk to Mr. White, but Mr. White said he couldn't understand him because Jeffrey stuttered—so he told him to get lost. Jeffrey just smiled and kept coming back. Every time he saw Mr. White, Jeffrey would tell him in a chopped-up way that he wanted to be the batboy. Mr. White would say no, he was too old, the Browns had enough batboys, anything he could think of, but nothing stopped Jeffrey.

Finally, to get Jeffrey to go away once and for all, Mr. White brought him into his office and explained to him that he just couldn't hire him, even if he wanted to. There was no more batboy uniforms, and even if there was one, it would be too small for Jeffrey. He told him it would be too dangerous with all those bats and balls flying around, and the Browns would lose their insurance. He give Jeffrey a Browns cap, a autographed baseball and a bum's rush out of the office. Next day, Jeffrey was back at the gate smiling like a drunk mule, wearing his cap, and asking to be the batboy.

Mr. White sent somebody to fetch him, and he give him the job of "keeper of the pitching jacket." Jeffrey's responsibility was to make sure the pitcher got his jacket when he wasn't pitching.

When they give Jeffrey a old uniform to wear, he lit up like a flare. Jeffrey loved baseball so much and loved the players so much that it rubbed off and reminded the players how much they loved the game and cared about each other. Mr. White said he started to enjoy managing, which he didn't realize he'd quit *enjoying* about fifty years ago. Whatever Jeffrey had, the whole team caught it.

They started winning. It just came natural. And toward the end of the season, even though he was as close to a pennant as he'd ever been, Mr. White said it didn't mean the same thing that it had. It was the games and the team that meant something to him.

Mr. White said it wasn't a coincidence that he won the pennant the same year he did something nice. I knew what he meant. Things turned out better for him than they did for me, but how things turn out don't have nothing to do with nothing, don't you see?

I've had a thousand choices to make in my time. It took me twenty-three years to figure out that a fellow's got little control as to whether a choice he makes turns out to be the right one. All he can do is make sure he done it for the right reason. And there's not but one reason. Same one why your mama sat up with you when you had the croup; same one why your pappy rubbed your head when he come home; same one why you let your dog lick you on the mouth. Love, is all.

I taught that Japanese boy how to pitch. It might have been the wrong decision, but it was for the right reason. If I had it to do over again, I would.

I thank you for giving me the chance to tell my side and for listening. Whatever happens, I hold no hard feelings. I hope the Army don't, neither. So long, Major.

Gooseball Flies Again

WASHINGTON, Sept. 4, 1966 (MNS) — Major league baseball and the U.S. Air Force took a long overdue step to correct a twenty-year-old injustice when they co-sponsored a Fan Appreciation Day for Andrew Jackson "Gooseball" Fielder before the Yankees-Senators game today.

As a rookie reliever for the St. Louis Browns during the 1941 American League pennant race, Fielder became an overnight sensation throwing his patented "gooseball," described by one contemporary sportswriter as an "underhand riser-curve."

His instant fame turned to infamy just as quickly when he balked home the winning run for the Yankees in the Browns' final game of the '41 season. Fielder's balk gave the American League pennant to the Yanks, who went on to take the World Series from Brooklyn.

Along with DiMaggio's 56-game hitting streak and Williams' .406 batting average, Fielder's fatal mistake made 1941 one of the most memorable years in baseball.

Following the bombing of Pearl Harbor later that year, Fielder enlisted in the then Army Air Corps, becoming a gunner on a B-29. Highly publicized allegations of treasonous conduct while a prisoner of war in Japan resulted in Fielder being blacklisted by the major leagues in 1946. Although a formal investigation conducted by the Army found no substance to the allegations, Fielder was never again allowed to play professional baseball.

Commissioner of Baseball William D. Eckert, retired lieutenant general of the Air Force, is credited with having arranged the ceremonies, which included presenting Fielder with an apology and the Air Force Medal of Valor. Also on hand for the ceremonies were Vice President Hubert H. Humphrey; Governor Orval E. Faubus of Arkansas, Fielder's home state; Mayor Ernest Musso of Toledo, Ohio, Fielder's mentor earlier in 1941 when they played for the Toledo Mudhens; and a number of teammates from the 1941 St. Louis Browns.

Fielder, now 44 and somewhat heavier than his playing weight, evoked a hearty laugh from the capacity crowd when he stumbled in the middle of delivering the opening pitch, a move reminiscent of the infamous balk immortalized in familiar newsreel footage. He received a standing ovation when he delivered a reasonable facsimile of his gooseball into the strike zone to start the game.

Also in attendance was Fielder's 24-year-old adopted son and namesake, Andrew Jackson Fielder II, who just completed a successful third season with the Yankees' AA farm club in Columbus after an All-American stint at the University of Arkansas.

When asked for a reaction to his son pitching one day for the Browns' archrival, the Yankees, Fielder said, "I spent all those years trying to teach him how to throw my gooseball and I reckon I ought to have been teaching him how to keep better company."

RICK NORMAN, an attorney in Lake Charles, Louisiana, played baseball in college before it was discovered—and repeatedly proven—that he could not hit a good curveball. Author of a 1983 treatise on corporate law, former federal prosecutor, and lecturer on the legal seminar circuit, Mr. Norman has always enjoyed storytelling and became a trial lawyer so that he might be paid for exaggerating.